CASSIUS
GOD OF THE SEAS

JAXON CHARLTON

Interior formatting by True North Book Interior Design

ISBN: 9798349551451

Acknowledgments

This book would not have been possible without the help of many, many people. The first is Shawn R. Charlton, my dad. I talked his ear off time and time again with ideas for this story. Secondly is David Trotter. Without his mentorship, publishing this story would be impossible. His friendship and expertise has been an inspiration to me for years on end.

It goes without saying that Aaron Moschner has been a huge part of making this story possible. His art has breathed a new layer of life into these words. He has worked for many hours to make the cover art, chapter headers, and maps that are found in this book. I owe him my deepest gratitude for all of his efforts in this project.

The next thanks goes to everyone who provided feedback during the drafting stages of writing this book. First, thanks to my alpha readers: Shawn Charlton, Nathan Cunningham, Ellie Drees, Bethannie Johnson, Olivia Johnson, Levi Landers, Becca McCulloch, and David Trotter. Of course, I can't forget the beta readers either: Melinda Cater, Shawn Charlton, Randy Haggart, Becca McCulloch, and David Trotter. Thanks to everyone who was willing to read this story when it was rough around the edges and unfinished! Your feedback was vital in making Cassius, God of the Seas the best it could possibly be.

Finally, I want to thank all of the family, friends, teachers, and people who supported me in my journey. This has been a long time coming, and it wouldn't have been possible without everyone who's been at my side over the years to encourage me and provide me with everything I've needed to grow as a person and a writer.

PELAGIOS
OTHENAI
TALASIA
HESTIA
ITHALE

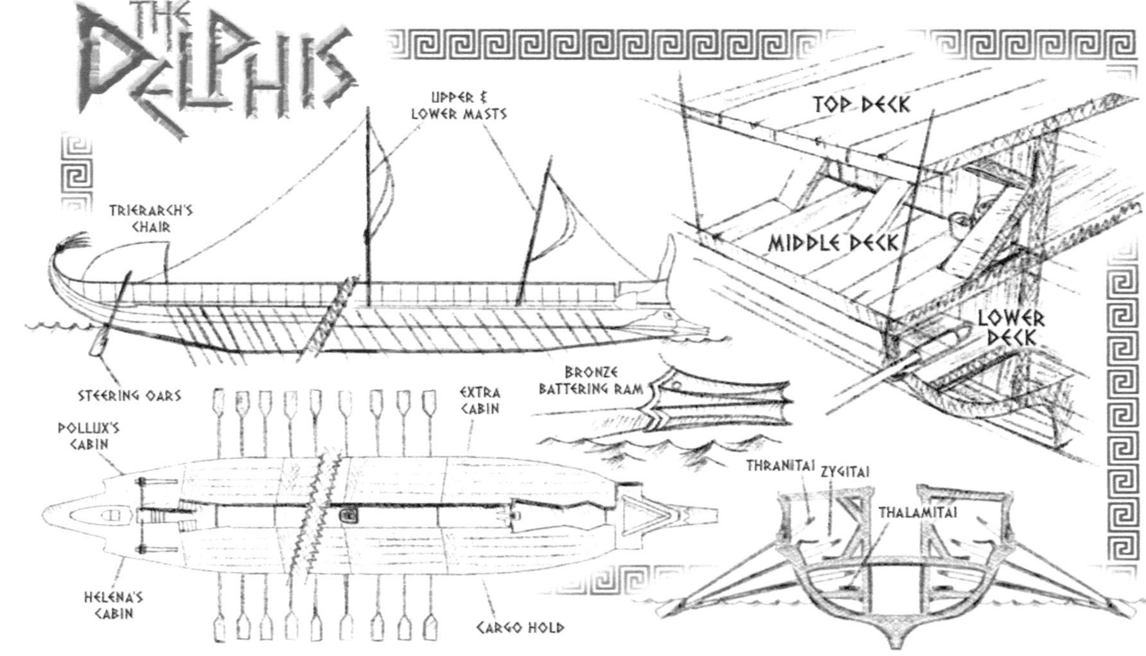

THE DELPHIS
UPPER & LOWER MASTS
TRIERARCH'S CHAIR
TOP DECK
MIDDLE DECK
LOWER DECK
STEERING OARS
EXTRA CABIN
BRONZE BATTERING RAM
POLLUX'S CABIN
THRANITAI ZYGITAI
THALAMITAI
HELENA'S CABIN
CARGO HOLD

CASSIUS

GOD of the SEAS

Prologue

Phoebe, goddess of passion, knew that something was wrong when her stomach started to ache. She understood that for humans it was a typical, if not common, occurrence, but for a goddess it could only mean something dire. In search of Zinnon, the king of gods, Phoebe strode the streets of Hestia, her beauty drawing the attention of every citizen. Where she was typically very concerned with her appearance, Phoebe paid no mind to her messy hair as she scurried through a vibrant market with her blush chiton held up off the ground.

"Goddess!" shouted a man from behind, interrupting Phoebe's flight through the city.

She turned her head to look over her shoulder. The crowd had parted, and the man stood with his hand outstretched, a bronze ring shimmering on his finger. His white chiton was stained with dirt that matched the tone of his dark hair.

"Yes?" Phoebe said.

The man lowered his hand and took a deep breath, his cheeks flushing red upon meeting Phoebe's gaze. "There's been a crime."

"Of what nature?" The pitiless twisting in her gut urged her onward to seek Zinnon's wisdom. She *shouldn't* feel this way. Yet somehow she felt a sort of kinship to the man.

His lip quivered as he met Phoebe with eyes that showed only horror. "My home was robbed and ransacked."

Phoebe spun away from the petitioner. "Find the hoplites. I have business elsewhere."

He grabbed her by the arm, his ring cold against her skin. "Goddess, please! They took my son."

Glancing down at his grip on her, Phoebe considered reducing him to dust before regaining clarity of mind. What if this man also had a stomach ache? Should he ignore his other worries in search of an apothecary? Phoebe considered that perhaps random pains were but one piece in the whole that was existence. In such a case, her stomach ache would reveal much about the passion of humanity. Even as a perfected god, Phoebe found herself curious as to the workings of the mortals. Sudden pity filled Phoebe, a wave of emotion that she was unprepared for. Her heart ached. "Your name?" She said.

He bowed his head. "Kleptes."

"You have your wish, Kleptes." Phoebe turned her chin upward. "Show me."

"Thank you." Without a second's pause, he rushed off down a street lined by marble villas with lush courtyards. Phoebe followed behind at a saunter, suppressing a grimace at the dull burning inside of her. After a short time, Kleptes turned down a narrower path then stopped in front of a shabby home. Its foundation matched the marble of Hestia, only it was chipped in places and covered in mosses of various shades of brown. The rest of the house was constructed of timber with paint that had long started to peel away.

Phoebe raised an eyebrow. "The robbers vandalized your home?"

Kleptes scratched the back of his neck and looked down at a crack in the paved stone underfoot. "I am a sailor by trade," he said. "My time for upkeep is limited."

"Never have I met a sailor as well spoken as you are."

"Cassius surely has."

Phoebe rolled her eyes. Only because of Cassius' aloofness were people like Kleptes superstitious about him. If they really met him, they would know him for the lost child he was. Without further conversation, Phoebe motioned for Kleptes to show her inside. He crossed the stony walkway and opened the door. "I would be a fool to enter before you have, goddess."

The inside of Kleptes' home shocked Phoebe as much as the outside had. The only furnishing, a woven couch, leaned to the side as it was missing a leg. Even the hearth showed no sign of recent use, a rarity during Sapila, the season of rot. "What purpose would ruining your home serve the thieves?" Phoebe paused in the center of the room and waved her hand. She reached for the magic contained inside of her but found the usual well nearly depleted. Reaching for the last drops, Phoebe felt the pain in her stomach fade. Curious. Was this mortal pain connected to the missing magic? Phoebe needed to finish this errand and receive Zinnon's council. She summoned an illuminating blaze in the hearth, which revealed a layer of dust covering the floor, undisturbed save for where Phoebe had already walked. If the house had been ransacked, why hadn't the robbers left tracks?

Something hard thudded against her head, and her vision went black.

Phoebe, goddess of passion, knew that something was wrong when she awoke with a headache. She understood that for humans it was a typical, if not common, occurrence, but for a goddess it could only mean something dire. The pain pounded the sides of her skull as if being driven in like a stake. A goddess should not be able to have a headache, much less be rendered unconscious by a liar and left in a pitch black room. Phoebe extended her will to its fullest and drew upon magic more distant than it should be. Her headache vanished, and she dissolved the bands. She stood, grabbing the edge of a table disguised within the darkness. Her head turned woozy. Phoebe stumbled, half-toppling over the table as she clutched the sides of her head.

Muffled thumps sounded outside. Instinct took hold, and Phoebe drew magic. Hands buzzing with energy, she clenched her teeth against the rage rising within. She felt around the dark room and found the door, pushing it open.

In the main room of the decrepit house, Kleptes stood in a circle with another man and a woman. Upon seeing Phoebe, Kleptes' eyes went wide, and he dashed for the door. With the flick of a finger, Phoebe caused a discarded board to fly over and bar the exit. "You thought to hurt me?" She said through clenched teeth.

Kleptes and the others edged away from Phoebe, drawing knives from their belts. "Forgive us, goddess," Kleptes said. "We meant nothing by it."

With a scoff, Phoebe glanced to the hearth, which still crackled with the fire she'd lit. The bright light reared against her headache, stinging deep within her head. She grimaced. There was no time for heretics.

Another of the thieves crouched down and set her knife on the ground. She had short hair and a cowlick that stuck up on the side of her head. "Let us be on our way, and you will never have to see us again."

"Mercy?" Phoebe felt tension return to her shoulders as she took a seething step forward, driving her foot into the ground. Her eyes fell on Kleptes. His hands shook as they held the jagged knife in front of him. "You petitioned me just to lead me into a trap. You took advantage of my honor—my kindness. For what?"

Kleptes' lip trembled, but he gave no attempt at reply.

"Answer me." Phoebe approached him, knowing that he wouldn't dare test her temper again.

"I...We thought to ransom you. Force the gods to barter for you at the Festival of Thriamvos."

Phoebe snorted. "I thought you were thieves or criminals," she said, "But here I find only fools." She turned her back on Kleptes and took a seat on the half broken couch. "There will be a punishment for your blasphemy. Justice demands that false worship be satisfied by way of ritual." No one dared speak against her. A thin smile stretched across Phoebe's lips, and she reached deep, forcing out the magic within. The fire in the hearth shifted from orange to radiant gold. "You will offer a sacrifice."

"We will give you anything," the woman said. "What do you ask of us?"

"You made a mockery of me." Phoebe closed her eyes. "Now you will be my most devoted disciples. You will give your lives to me in service."

A chill fell over the room. With her eyes shut, Phoebe could not see as the thieves were lured to the flame by her spell. She smelt the dust displaced by their forced steps. While they did not speak words, Phoebe heard the strain as they tried to break free from her enchantment. Still, whether they intended to or not, their bodies marched on. The first reached the hearth and stepped into the blaze. The screams began, accompanied by the scent of burnt flesh, but all Phoebe felt was annoyance at the waste of time.

Once the cries ended, Phoebe stood and took one look at the husk left in the hearth. She snuffed out the fire with a thought then left the house to continue her search for Zinnon. Outside, the sun was setting on the horizon, draping long ribbons of orange light over the valley. While she did draw the attention of citizens once more, Phoebe ignored their looks and comments as she crossed the city to Hestia's famous port. Earlier, the servants at Zinnon's temple said that he had traveled to the port to broker peace between the fleets of Kleos and Perseo. Upon her arrival, Phoebe found the port peaceful and quiet as most of the sailors and fishermen had already left. The familiar rolling of the tide helped to soothe the tightness that she was still carrying in her back and hands. She walked until she found Zinnon walking down a dock. At its end sat Cassius, god of the seas and most cowardly of them all.

"I thought I sensed you here," Zinnon said. "Something troubles you, Phoebe."

She nodded. "I...woke up this morning with a stomach ache."

"I see." Zinnon's face did not show the surprise she expected. "Uncomfort is a curse that even we are not above."

Phoebe exhaled softly and steeled herself. On the way to the docks, she had time to think about the aches in her body and the difficulty in using her magic. Even the thieves' ease in knocking her out seemed a clue to her malady. "I thought we were magic itself," she said, "But that's wrong. We only use it to make ourselves gods. I think today I started to run out."

Zinnon pursed his lips behind his curly white beard. "I see you have remembered our origin."

"I'm right then?"

"You are close. We ourselves are as ancient as the cosmos itself, but our presence on Pelagios requires a binding of sorts."

Something stirred within Phoebe, and she knew that Zinnon was right. Though there was more she was missing. It all felt...unnatural for whatever reason. She looked down the dock to Cassius sitting on its edge, his feet in the water. "I didn't act as I normally do. It got me into some trouble."

Zinnon nodded. "Without magic, you were as the mortals, swayed by their weaknesses."

Phoebe looked out at the Minean Sea. The Union drew her toward Cassius where he sat. "I'll be at your palace in a moment."

"Do not reveal what you have learned," Zinnon said. "This is a secret we bear even from our siblings."

She paused for a moment. "I will keep it for now. We can discuss this further in your palace." Phoebe left Zinnon behind.

As she approached, Cassius looked back at Phoebe, the sunsets reflecting off his blonde curls. "So I'm not the only one who is early."

Phoebe nodded. "I came for the wisdom of Zinnon."

"You'll find far less in me." Cassius turned his gaze back to the Minean Sea, his hands on the edge of the dock as he leaned out over the surf.

The Union inside urged Phoebe closer to Cassius. She sat next to him, their elbows touching. "I had a stomach ache today," she said. "Then a headache."

"I'm sorry, sister." Cassius' blue eyes sparkled in the same way that light rippled off the surface of water. Looking into them, Phoebe could see the care that he tried so hard to lock away. "Is it better now?"

Phoebe nodded. "The pain is gone, but...to be truthful, I'm terrified."

Silent gaze fixed on her face, he wiped the sweat of his palms on his chiton.

"We're supposed to be perfect," said Phoebe.

"Are we?" He tilted his head sideways for a moment then returned to the sea before them. "There." Cassius pointed out into the horizon. A dark shape blurred, leaping out of the water then splashing back down. Others followed, racing across the waves. "Dolphins," Cassius said with a smile.

Phoebe frowned. She didn't know what she had expected from Cassius, but she supposed it shouldn't have been much more than this.

"I wonder too what all of this means." Cassius raised his eyes to the emerging stars above. "I feel...small compared to the vastness of everything."

A lump formed in Phoebe's throat as she realized that she'd been wrong. Cassius did understand how she felt. Perhaps that explained his irresponsibility. Phoebe would not allow herself to become so lazy. She would find the answers, and with them the truth of her role as goddess of passion.

ACT I
ROARING TEMPEST

The sea that did twist
And struggle to find its light
Ever becoming

Chapter One

From his seat at the table of the gods, Cassius, god of the seas, gazed out at the festival spread across the valley. Humans worshiped Cassius and his siblings, celebrating the beginning of Thriamvos, the first in a new cycle of seasons and festival of triumph, new beginnings, and the harvest. Of all the seasons, Thriamvos was the most celebrated. Dotted around the valley were eighteen colorful banners, one for each of the gods. Forming a neat arc around the temple of Zinnon where the gods sat were the six banners of the gods of human emotions and experiences. The banners of the lesser gods spread across the valley wherever the gods' followers met. Cassius' banner, cobalt blue and adorned with a black seahorse, stood at a small fishing shack near the city's port, alone and devoid of worshipers. Likely, one of Zinnon's servants hung the banner as no one else would have bothered.

"It's okay, Cassius," Oura, the goddess of the skies, whispered to Cassius. "I don't have very many worshipers either." She pointed to her banner, a light blue depiction of the sun shining through clouds. Beneath it, nearly a hundred men and women flew kites and burned offerings to the goddess. As they watched, Oura smiled and rested a hand on Cassius' arm, her feathered gray dress and long brown hair swaying in the breeze.

Cassius looked at himself in the reflection of the polished

marble table to see if he shared any of Oura's lightness. He found blonde hair parted down the middle, a sharp jawline, and eyes empty of anything but the blue of the sea. Like the other gods, he was beautiful, far more than a mortal, but he hadn't shared that same god-like glow with his siblings for many years now.

How could he? Of all the gods, he was the one most hated by mortals. A long time ago, he had been as generous as the rest. However, over the centuries, Cassius realized that every time he tried to help, he only ruined lives further. It seemed easier to let nature run its course without his intervention. The mortals didn't need him anyways.

"Hey, Cassius!" a voice boomed from the other side of the table. Kleos, the god of glory, laughed as he called out to Cassius, a long scar stretching from the middle of his forehead across, his right eye, and onto the jaw of his battle-hardened face. Kleos healed the eye after the battle, but left the scar for the glory of being injured in battle. The war deity wore a set of leather and bronze armor, a red cape hanging from one shoulder and two servants flanking behind him to carry his helmet and sword. He was one of the deities of experience, the greater gods. Of course, in the grand scheme of the universe and its magic, all gods were equal, but Zinnon and the others had put themselves in power as the leaders of the gods in a time so far away that not even Cassius could remember it. "Are you done making that dumb face yet? We're trying to celebrate here, have some fun!"

Cassius wiped the sweat of his palms on the cloth of his chiton, a long white robe he wore under his blue himation. The himation was more of a cloak that wrapped across one shoulder. As the weakest of the gods, the others had developed a habit of picking on Cassius, Kleos especially. Once Zinnon showed up, he'd be safe. Until then, they'd do everything in their power to get under his skin. "Hey, Kleos,"

Cassius said, "I was admiring your warship in the harbor this morning. It's the largest I've ever seen."

"Makes you wonder what he's trying to hide," Perseo, the god of boldness, said across the table from Kleos. His chiton was cut and bound just above his hips, leaving his chest uncovered save for a forest green himation.

Between Kleos and Perseo, Phoebe giggled, her dark curls bouncing as she laid a hand on Kleos' knee. As the goddess of passion, Phoebe's beauty exceeded that of anyone Cassius had ever met. Her green eyes perfectly matched the laurel crown woven around her head and the form fitting chiton wrapping across her body. She always seemed to entertain Kleos and Perseo's games, though she never participated. Of all the gods, Phoebe was the closest with the mortals, her interest in their stories driving her to interact with them more than the others did. A crystal bowl of glowing mushrooms sat at the center of the table, illuminating the gods in colorful light. While the mushrooms were a powerful source of light for gods and mortals alike, they were not particularly tasty.

"Shut up, Perseo." Kleos turned back to Cassius, rolling his dark eyes. "Brings up a good point though. You sank eight of my ships this season and six of Phoebe's." He waved at Perseo across the table, who still had a grin stretched across his face. "This fool only lost one ship. Seems unfair."

Cassius blushed and stumbled over an apology. "It's no fault of my own," he said. "Perseo just uses better technique than you do."

"What?" Kleos rose from his chair. Beside him, Phoebe tried to hide her amusement at the outburst. Behind him, his servants stepped forward with his weapons, as if expecting a battle to break out.

"It's simple," Perseo gave Cassius a knowing look, as if thanking him for the moment, "My men are trained in sailing and war. Sure, yours can fight, but they can't do the rest of the work it takes to win a war."

Slinking back into his chair, Cassius glanced at the golden doors to Zinnon's palace looming ominously behind the table. In front of the doors sat his massive throne, imposing as ever. Zinnon was both the god of enlightenment and the king of the gods. He acted as a father to the rest of them, but as far as Cassius could remember, Zinnon wasn't any older or more magical than any of the gods. Still, looking at Zinnon's austere golden throne, he could feel the connection inside of him that all the gods had. They called it the Union, but rarely talked about it. Even for them, it felt too holy to speak of in passing.

Beneath the dais on which the gods sat, humans began to walk up and ask for blessings. A man asked for his village to be protected from a plague that was creeping through the rainforest. A group of hunters petitioned Kleos for strength in capturing a wild beast. Soldiers, families, merchants, and more approached and asked for blessing after blessing. Cassius simply sat back and picked at his food, sipping at his glass of wine and hoping for as little trouble as possible.

As Cassius waited for the festival to end, a family caught his eye. A father, mother, and their daughters, all wearing white himations, paused a few meters away from the dais. The father knelt down and kissed his daughter on the forehead before gesturing at her with strange motions of his hands. Cassius knew the family. They lived in Talasia, the city state he ruled over. They had to have traveled days by boat to get to Hestia. The father stood, taking his daughter's hand in his as he stepped up to the dais, making direct eye contact with Cassius.

"Lord Cassius," he said, bowing his head. "Please, bless my daughter, Mya. She was born without the ability to hear. She is happy, but... how much happier could she be?" His face showed the wrinkles and weariness of a lifetime working on docks. Like all humans, he could never compare in the luster and beauty of the gods. His daughter, on the other hand, might have a chance. Mya had an innocent face and a bright smile, her light hair tied back behind her head with a thin piece of cord.

All of the other gods at the table turned toward Cassius, eyes wide as they waited for his reply. He froze, searching for the right words and actions, but too afraid of saying or doing the wrong thing. What if he embarrassed himself? Worse, what if he did the wrong thing and only made this man's daughter more unhappy?

He waved his hand, averting his eyes away from the hand and calling over a servant. A young servant girl rushed over. "Yes, my lord?"

"Bring me wine."

"As you wish." She whisked away, her chiton brushing against the floor. Cassius stared down at his hands, ignoring the family and hoping that they would leave. He ignored them until a horn blew and the doors to Zinnon's palace swung open. The commanding god walked out with his head held high, curly white beard as perfect as ever. Servants flooded the dais with more food and drinks. Below, mortals rushed forward to seek blessings from Zinnon, the greatest of gods. Mya and her father disappeared into the crowd's pleas for help. Even if Cassius wanted to help, there was nothing to be done now but to try and survive a long, long day of celebrations.

Chapter Two

Two days later, once the festivities had ended and people were returning to their normal lives, Cassius sat atop a green hill in Hestia with the gods who hadn't returned to their homes yet. Each of the gods ruled over a city state. Hestia, the home of the gods, belonged to Zinnon and was the place where the gods came together at the start of each season to feast together and bless the humans.

Except for Cassius. He'd been too afraid to help Mya. That night, Cassius had tossed and turned in bed until finally, he gave up and paced the docks of Hestia instead. He lost himself in the memory of his shortcomings until the sun rose again on the horizon. Now, the gods lounged on the hill together, playing games and laughing with one another as fluffy clouds drifted through the blue sky. Cassius sat off to the side tossing olives into his mouth and watching as Phoebe and Kleos played a game where they threw bronze discus across a large field and made their servants go and retrieve them.

"Is it true that you and Perseo have chosen peace for this cycle?" Phoebe said.

Kleos shrugged, an awkward motion in his armor. "It is. Regardless, I am ready for the worst. I have laid traps in all of the seas surrounding Ithale."

"Oh, did you? I don't suppose you'll tell me what those are." Phoebe wore her hair braided behind her head and a shorter himation that allowed her to move more freely.

"You hear that, Zinnon?" Kleos said, giving the king of gods a knowing look. Zinnon sat under a makeshift pavilion of tarp and logs with a pile of books his servants had brought him. He sighed and sat up from his thin mattress to see what Kleos wanted. "She's trying to steal my secrets. I think she's working with Perseo!"

Cassius held his breath and looked over at the king of the gods. The gods were technically equal in power, but Zinnon had always held himself differently. There was an authority to him that none of the other gods had ever shared. Some even guessed that Zinnon was the only remaining god to remember Ktisis, the creation of the world. He'd be the only one that could, since the memory was far too distant for Cassius and the other gods to recall.

Zinnon grumbled and stood up. "You are not good at this game." He grabbed a discus from their pile. "Discus is a game of strength, yes. But it's also a game of rhythm." Zinnon held the discus in front of him between his hands before pulling it back to his side with a single hand, holding it from the top. He repeated this motion several times before he finally released, sending the discus in a gentle, shimmering arc down the hill and across the field, further than anyone else had thrown. Even Cassius sat up taller to see how far it would travel.

As he watched the discus finally hit the ground, Kleos' face flushed red and he stamped the grass beneath his foot. Phoebe only laughed and tried the technique for herself. As they spoke, Kleos' champion approached with arms full of the recovered discus. He stared at Phoebe with longing eyes, puffing his chest and setting his jaw as he lay down the discus by her bare feet. The goddess batted her eyes at him, but he only bowed his head, dark hair covering his forehead. Every so often, Kleos chose a champion from his worshipers. It was always someone who had proven themselves in battle. Once chosen, they embarked on special quests in Kleos' honor.

"Ah, Damian,"–Kleos rested a hand on the champion's shoulder–"you are exactly what I need." He turned back to Phoebe. "Do you suppose that your servants can catch the discus better than my champion?"

Phoebe and Zinnon shared an amused look. Rolling his eyes, Zinnon returned to his seat and opened a new book. A discus hovered up from the pile, a red swirl of magic trailing beneath it. As it landed in her hand, Phoebe winked at Damian. "Sure," she said, waving one of her own servants down the hill.

"Go fetch, Damian." Both of the mortals ran off. Once they were a ways down, Kleos and Phoebe threw their discs. They arced nicely down the grassy hillside, each on target for the representative of their respective god. Just as Kleos' discus reached Damian's outstretched hands, Cassius tapped the well of magic inside of the Union, moving the discus just inches out of the champion's reach. A few paces away from him, Phoebe's servant caught her discus and leapt in celebration. The gods on the hill laughed at Kleos and Damian.

Fists clenched at his side, Kleos stormed over to one of his hoplites, a soldier wearing bronze armor and carrying a javelin. "You!" He said before jabbing a finger toward the figure of Damian below. "Tear him to pieces!"

The hoplite rushed off, and Phoebe giggled as her own servant climbed up the hill. "It seems I've won, Kleos."

The god of glory crossed his arms, eyes locked on the boy below. Damian had tried to run, but Cassius could feel Kleos' magic stop his legs from working. "Kleos," Cassius said, "let him go. I used magic to move the discus. It's not his fault."

"I will not tolerate weakness."

"He is only weak in the wake of gods." Cassius stood and grabbed Kleos' elbow. The god only shrugged him away. At the base of the hill, Damian had drawn his sword to face the hoplite. "Do not let your vanity end his life."

"You did this, so you will watch as I feed the boy's body to crows. Then, I will declare war on you and destroy your people."

With a sigh, Cassius reached into the Union. Using magic, he drew water from the ground, pulling it through the dirt and creating a bubble around Damian. He lifted the boy high into the air. In seconds, Damian flew across the city and landed on Cassius' ship at the docks of Hestia. "Do not punish your own servant for what I did."

"Fine." Kleos grabbed Cassius by his himation, tearing it as he drew Cassius in. Teeth clenched, he said the next part in a low growl. "You will feel my wrath, lost child. You will regret the day you made me look weak before the king of gods." Sweat formed on Cassius' palms as he pulled himself away. He couldn't find the right words to say as Kleos stomped away, a squadron of hoplites following close behind him.

Chapter Three

A week later, Cassius sat on the old pier on his beach in Talasia, torn pants pulled up to his knees so he could dangle his feet in the water. Behind him stood his little hut, a shoddy building with more character than substance. Further down the beach, children laughed and played while their parents worked within the city. Gray clouds covered the sun, and the familiar earthy scent of a storm brewing blew in from the Minean Sea. Despite the dreary sky and rough sea, children laughed as they competed in foot races and tossed around a ball fashioned from animal hide.

Talasia, Cassius' city state, was home to the largest port in the world. As far as the eye could see, docks stretched into the Minean, housing some of the greatest triremes the oceans had ever seen. At the docks of Talasia, hard working men and women built and repaired vessels of all kinds. Most of these left for the merchant routes as soon as they were finished. Over the past several seasons, the port had mainly built war vessels for the series of conflicts between Perseo and Kleos.

From where he sat, Cassius could see the ongoing construction of *The Delphis*. Commissioned by Zinnon's followers to establish his dominance in the Minean, *The Delphis* was designed to be the grandest ship on the sea with three rows of oars along either side and a curved bronze ram jutting from the bow. Men climbed the masts, attaching white canvases to either side as they ascended towards the crows nest. In only a few days, it would be ready to sail. Cassius couldn't help but admire it. Once it led a fleet of its own, *The Delphis* would create legends spoken of for centuries to come.

Kleos had yet to fulfill his promise of war, but Cassius knew it would come. He only wondered when he should warn the people of Talasia and if they would trust him. What reason had he given them? Every time they asked for help, he found a reason not to. Part of him wanted to, but there was always the fear of what may happen if he somehow messed it up, again. Saving Damian had only confirmed this fear. Sure, he'd rescued Damian from being killed, but how many would die at Kleos' might when he attacked the city?

On the beach, a man appeared out of the sea, striding through the tide as if he'd been hiding underwater all along. His eyes glowed golden and his head was bald save for a curly white beard. He wore a pristine chiton and himation, both perfectly dry despite the water. "Hello, children," Zinnon said to the kids playing on the beach. They stared in awe, trans-fixed by the grandeur of the king of gods. Only one girl stood apart, jumping over waves and giggling. She was Mya, the deaf girl from the festival. Zinnon only gave her a pitied look before joining Cassius on his pier.

"Father." Cassius bowed his head as Zinnon climbed the steps. "I did not expect you to come to collect *The Delphis* so early."

"My ship can wait." Zinnon's words were drawn out and as melancholic as the gray clouds painted across the sky. His gaze fixed upon the horizon. "This is about you, my lost child."

"What is it?" Cassius slouched down and the lapping sea seemed colder than it was before. He reached into the Union to feel Zinnon's soul, which ached from grief. It seemed whatever the king of gods had come to say, it pained him in a way only gods could feel.

Zinnon returned his attention to Cassius, his eyes full of pity. "Did you watch as she played? So full of life, but so alone. She is human, but she cannot be like them."

"Mya?" Cassius looked over to where the other kids had continued their footraces. Mya tried to join in, bouncing with excitement. Another child counted down, but Mya could not hear and started late each time once she saw the boy beside her begin to run. Over and over again, she lost. Apparently, none of the other children had learned to speak to her using hand signals like her parents.

"What joys are lost to her? She will never hear the seagulls call or the loving voice of her mother." Zinnon's essence reached out to Cassius in the Union, sharing his feelings of sadness. The emotion became as real in Cassius as it was in Zinnon and it felt as though they became one being, united in thought and purpose. "Don't you see?" Zinnon said, the words soft against his lips. "She could be so much more."

"Yes," Cassius said, closing his eyes to allow the salty sea breeze to bring its comfort to him like it always had.

"So why didn't you save her?"

The moment of clarity ended, and a tightness formed in Cassius' chest. "Zinnon, you have to understand, I wanted to."

"No." Thunder rumbled on the horizon. Cassius stood up, his pants dripping water onto the pier. "We are gods, Cassius. We are *order*. The world was organized by our design. If we want something, we have it. Nothing stops us. That is why the mortals need us."

"But what if they didn't? What if they could be happy without our hand?"

Zinnon pursed his lips and rain began to fall from above. "Ah," he said, "so this is about Antia."

A bitter taste filled Cassius' mouth. Many cycles ago, he'd fallen in love with a mortal named Antia. He'd given her everything, but she left him anyway. After that, he stopped blessing the mortals. They seemed better off without him anyways. His fingers twitched as his mind recalled seeing Antia for the last time. A shiver ran up his spine.

"You must learn a lesson." Zinnon placed his hands on Cassius' shoulders and closed his eyes, taking in a deep breath.

"What are you doing?"

"Only what is necessary for you to understand the role of the gods." A wall appeared in the Union, blocking Cassius from the magic. His connection to the other gods vanished, but he could still feel Zinnon's essence close. A tear fell down Zinnon's cheek as he stepped away. "I wish you well, my lost child. One day, when you have learned, we will be reunited. I hope then you understand why I have to let this happen." Golden light shimmered around Zinnon.

"Wait!" Cassius raised a hand to shield his eyes from the light. The sound of electricity crackled through the air, and the king of gods dissipated into orange mist. Out of instinct, Cassius tried to reach into his soul to speak to the gods, but the barrier held strong. Weight pressed down on his shoulders, and Cassius ran into his hut as his body began to transform into that of a mortal. He felt swelling in his arms and legs. His sandy hair fell into his eyes. An ache formed in his stomach. Cassius curled up on his mattress, whispering a plea for help.

Then the nausea came. Cassius leaned over the edge of his mattress, trying to hold back vomit as tears streamed from his eyes. A clammy rush of blood surged through his body as he trembled. He could feel as his bones shrank inside of his body and his skin loosened around his frame. Pain racked through his shoulders and down his spine. All Cassius could do as the tingling reverberated through his body was close his eyes and hope for an end.

Chapter Four

The next morning, Cassius threw open the door to a short wooden building where the city's seamstresses worked. He dashed through, finding a full length mirror on the far wall. As he stood there, holding both sides of the mirror, he blinked over and over again until he was sure that the image reflected back at him was real and not a hallucination.

His transformation into a mortal had taken at least a hand's width of height from him, and his chiton dragged against the floor where it had once hung above his ankles. He ran a finger along his jawline, now rounded and not nearly as pronounced as it had once been. Pimples marked his forehead and chin, ugly and red. Where his muscles had once been tight and rippling, his skin now sagged. A seamstress asked if he needed help, but all Cassius could see was the paleness of his face and arms. With every pant, it became more real to him that he'd met his fate.

Outside, warning bells began ringing throughout the city. The seamstresses rushed about, shutting the door and setting aside their work. An old woman grabbed Cassius and ushered him to a closet filled with fabric in the back of the building. "We need to hide. The city is under attack."

"Attack?" Cassius said, running a hand through his greasy hair.

"Don't you know the bells?" She paused to listen again. "Three hits of the lower tones. It's an attack by sea."

Cassius paused, remembering Kleos' fleet of ships at the festival. Had he finally come to fulfill his threat? If so, Cassius needed to stop him. He could even convince Kleos to help him regain his powers. "I need to go," Cassius said, pulling himself out of the closet, much to the dismay of the seamstresses. He ran out of the shop and down the street toward the port, his chest heaving in exhaustion. At the port, men and women bustled about, preparing for the worst.

A hundred or so strides out, several dozen ships with red masts approached the beaches. Armored hoplites cheered from the decks, spears and torches held high. Once the ships were in wading distance of the beach, the hoplites leapt down and rushed into the city. Chaos broke out as people abandoned the docked merchant vessels and ran for safety.

A chill ran down Cassius' spine as the sound of footsteps echoed behind him. He turned, holding his hands out to show that he wasn't a threat. Kleos marched towards him with a squadron of hoplites, a sword in one hand and a spear in the other. A crimson cape flowed behind him, matching the glow in his eyes. "So it is true, brother!" He cackled and rammed the butt of his spear into a crack in the cobblestone streets so it would stand on its own. "You have fallen."

Cassius' heart rate quickened and his hands began to sweat. "Kleos, please. It doesn't have to be this way."

"Tell me, do the mortals recognize you?"

Blood rushed to Cassius' ears and he could feel himself reddening. "Please, I need your help."

"But you don't deserve it." Kleos thumped a fist against his chest as a pair of soldiers approached with someone held between them. The prisoner looked up, blood dribbling from his nose. "Ah, Damian," Kleos said. "You made me look weak, stupid even. I will not stand for that." He slammed his fist into the boy's jaw. Damian fell over without a sound, laying there for a moment before pushing himself back to his knees to stare Kleos down. Kleos only laughed. "You're strong as ever, boy." Kleos brought up a knee into Damian's jaw, and the boy's head flew back. With the wave of his hand, Kleos healed Damian's body of its bruises. The beatdown began again. Soon, more soldiers had joined in. Each time, Kleos healed Damian, restarting the cycle of his pain. One last series of hits landed, leaving Damian bloodied and unconscious on the street. Still, his chest rose and fell with shallow breaths, the only sign of life remaining in him. Kleos stood over him, grinning wildly as blood dripped from his knuckles.

Another hoplite approached, a spear held in his white knuckled grip. "Lord Kleos,"–He knelt down on one knee and pulled his bronze helmet free to bow his head–"We have the girl. Aejac is taking her to your vessel."

"Good." Kleos turned back towards Cassius. "Now finish it."

The soldier stood and made his way toward the pier. "Burn them!" He shouted for all to hear. "Set fire to the ships!"

Cassius inched away, trying to lose Kleos' attention and run away. As the ships erupted in a blaze behind him, Kleos smiled, coming close enough that Cassius could smell the sour stench of his breath. "Do it," Kleos said. "I've hurt Damian. I've taken Mya. Run away, show them what kind of coward you are. Leave the glory for me." Cassius hesitated, his breath catching in his throat. Seeing Damian on the ground brought back painful memories. He'd tried to help the boy, but he'd failed. All he ever did was fail. Nothing would change that. Every time he tried to take a step, his foot trembled and he found himself too weak to even attempt it.

Kleos raised his spear in the air and roared in pleasure. He turned away and watched the flames dance around him, ashes smoldering at his feet. The god laughed as the mast of a boat crumbled, falling over and plunging into the sea below. Next to it, another ship split in half with a loud crack and began to sink. Fire ran down the planks of the port, pressing in and threatening to consume the city. Before Cassius could find the resolve to escape, Kleos placed a hand on his shoulder and attacked his soul. Without moving a muscle, Kleos slammed his essence into Cassius'. For a second, Cassius' heart forgot to beat and his lungs forgot to breathe as Kleos yanked his essence, twisting it and exhausting it of any strength that remained. His senses weakened until the world seemed cold and the only sound remaining was the ringing of his ears. Cassius stared up at Kleos just as Damian had a moment ago, but without any of the defiance. Only defeat remained.

"Tell me, Cassius," Kleos said. "Do you bleed?" He paused for a moment then rammed his spear into Cassius' gut. The god of glory's eyes grew wide and the corners of his lips turned into a frown for a second as he saw the spear jutting out of Cassius' body. Cassius clutched at the wound, his gut numb as he felt cool, viscous blood cover his fingers and hand. Then, as Cassius raised his hands to see the crimson blood, Kleos' mouth turned upward in a cruel grin.

"Please." Cassius nearly choked on the words.

Kleos stormed away, leaving his spear embedded in Cassius' stomach. He fell to his knees, pressing a hand against his wound and wincing at the pain. Hoplites flooded past, cheering for glory as they spit on Damian's unconscious body. Before he knew it, Cassius found himself lying on his back, staring at the lifeless buildings lining the inside of the port. Smoke burned his throat, nostrils, and eyes.

Some time later, a man appeared down the street, wearing pants and a button up shirt. The gods would have laughed at his sense of style. His long black hair was tied behind his head in a curly bun. A group of several dozen people followed behind him, carrying buckets and glowing mushrooms for light as they marched toward the docks. As the first man approached, his emerald green eyes locked onto Cassius. He rushed over and placed his hands on his chest. His touch somehow cooled Cassius' skin and numbed the pain where the spear jutted from his stomach. "You're alive," the man said beneath the crackle of the flames. "I can help you, but I need you to stay alive. Can you do that?"

Cassius opened his mouth, but as soon as he tried to speak, he coughed and pain racked through his body again. The stranger steadied him, static energy spreading from his fingertips. Cassius' eyes drooped and he found himself fading off into unconsciousness. Before he knew it, he fell asleep in the man's arms, forgetting his pain and all that had happened.

Chapter Five

Cassius awoke to the metallic scent of blood as the dark haired man removed his bandages. Fire burned across his ribs as the man applied some kind of paste to the wounds. Light shone into the room through a wooden shuddered window, revealing another bed next to Cassius' that was empty save for blood staining the wool sheets. Something about the man tending to him calmed Cassius. His pain faded as the paste oozed into his skin.

"How long?" Cassius said, the words harsh against his hoarse throat.

"The attack happened yesterday, if that's what you mean. It's about an hour from sunset now." The man began wrapping a linen bandage around the freshly cleaned wounds. "Do you remember what happened?"

"Sadly."

The man only laughed. He finished bandaging Cassius' wound then checked over his work with a satisfied smile, his emerald eyes glimmering against the daylight streaming in. "I'm Pollux by the way. I used to captain one of the merchant barges."

"Thank you for helping me," Cassius said. His eyelids drooped and he rested his head against the pillow. "How is the city?"

"Broken. There's a group of us meeting downstairs in a couple minutes to fix it. It's about time I head over."

"I want to come."

"You can't walk with your sutures."

"Suture? What is that supposed to mean?"

Pollux tilted his head. "I had to sew your wounds together with some fishing line to close it. It's so the skin heals back together." He scratched his head. "You really didn't know what a suture was?"

"No." Cassius used a hand to poke at the numb wound through his bandage. "So you're an apothecary?"

Pollux snorted. "You'd be better off with the crows than an apothecary." A knock came from the door and he swung it open. A woman with dark hair and tan skin stepped in, a grin on her heart-shaped face. In all, she was gorgeous for a mortal.

"Pollux!" She said, ignoring Cassius. "You're late. Even the kid beat you to the meeting and he almost looks as bad as this guy."

"I'm trying to keep him alive, Helena. The meeting can wait a few minutes."

Cassius coughed to get their attention. "And I'd have to say I appreciate it." Mustering all the strength he had, Cassius pushed himself upright with his hands. He winced, part of him wishing he'd stayed on the bed. "Now let's go. I'm tired of laying here."

"You've been unconscious," Helena said, raising an eyebrow. Her eyes were the exact same shade as Pollux's. Although her facial features were much softer, the two of them were unmistakable as siblings.

"She's right, you're in no shape to go to the meeting, even if it's just downstairs." Pollux's gaze remained locked on Cassius.

"I can make it," Cassius said. He wanted to know more

about what Kleos had done to the city, and how these people dared try and fix it. It was the only thing that seemed enough to distract him from his misery. "Besides," Cassius said, "why not just have it up here? There's plenty of room."

There was an instant understanding in Pollux's emerald eyes. Apparently, Cassius' determination had impressed him. With a sigh, he shook his head. "Fine," Pollux said. "Go tell everyone, Helena."

Without a word, Helena left the room. Pollux pulled the dirty sheets from the second bed and took them away, his footsteps echoing through the stone hallway. When he returned, he carried a stack of wooden stools. He set them out and took one, tapping his foot and whistling as he waited on the others. "You're hiding something," he said after a couple seconds.

Cassius blushed, avoiding eye contact with Pollux. "Aren't we all?" He said.

"You have a point," Pollux leaned back and rested against the wall. "One day I'll figure you out, just wait."

A few minutes later, Helena returned with a group of men and women. Cassius immediately recognized Damian, whose face was bruised purple. A sword hung from his side, but he unbuckled the scabbard and set it against the wall when he took a seat at the second bed. The only other people that Cassius recognized were Mya's parents, eyes red from crying. They stood close enough to one another that their elbows seemed tied together. The room silently filled until twenty or so people sat or stood against the walls, dark expressions on their faces.

"Thank you all for coming," Pollux said. "I'm sorry about the sudden change in location. It seems our friend here was also wronged by the war pig's men." He nodded to Cassius. The others only stared, soot still staining their faces. "Regardless, we can't wait to take action. Whatever we do, it must be decisive."

"We can't fight him," Damian said. "That's what he wants. In a head on fight, he'll win every time and he knows it."

"Then how do you expect to save my daughter?" Mya's father said, the words slurred. He clenched his fists. "You're the reason she's gone anyways. You and that fool of a god Cassius."

Cassius felt his ears grow hot. Still, no one seemed to notice him. He had yet to become accustomed to his new appearance. To everyone else, he was only a stranger they'd found in the fires the previous day. No one saw him as the god of the seas any longer.

"Calm, Daedus." Pollux sighed. "Damian has a point."

Mya's father, Daedus, huffed and swayed from foot to foot, glaring at Damian across the room. Damian shied away, looking down at the wooden floor.

"Are there any good options?" Helena said. She glanced at Pollux. "No one's ever warred against Kleos without the help of a god. Maybe we need to petition Cassius or even another one of the gods."

"No," Pollux said, his words as sturdy as an olive tree. "The gods have abandoned us. They are no good to us. We don't need their help." He paused. "But we can still use them against each other. Kleos and Perseo are at war too. What if we use that to our advantage?"

"Not anymore," Cassius said, remembering the agreement Kleos and Perseo had made at the festival. For the first time in many cycles, they'd made peace with one another. "Their war is over."

"How do you know?" Pollux scratched his neck.

"I overheard it yesterday. One of Kleos' men mentioned something like that before I was discovered." Cassius lied of course, but if anyone in the room knew his secret, they'd all hate him. He only wanted to regain his powers with as little hassle as possible and then get away from these mortal struggles. "There's another way though." Cassius took in all the gaunt and soot covered faces focused on him. He swallowed. "To hurt him, I mean."

"And what is that?"

"We'd have to get to Ithale. Damian can help us take the long way around. Kleos only monitors the direct path into the island's port, but there's a secret way through Othenai."

Everyone in the room turned to Damian for confirmation. He nodded slowly, eyes fixed on Cassius.

"But we can't do anything until we have a ship again. Did any survive the attack?"

"Only one," Pollux said. "*The Delphis*."

Of course, Kleos never would have burned Zinnon's ship. In fact, Cassius suspected that Kleos would've gone to rather extreme measures in order to protect it from harm. Zinnon would surely be angry if they took it. Cassius pushed aside his fear, eager for the chance to get back at Zinnon.

"That's the best plan we have," Pollux said. "We need a crew gathered by sundown. *The Delphis* disembarks at midday tomorrow." He set about organizing the people in the room, tasking each with a role in preparing the ship. Cassius lay there, staring at the ceiling when Pollux finally returned to him, sitting at the foot of his bed. "Who are you?"

"My name is Cass. I... I was a farmer further inland, but I came here a few seasons ago to start anew. I want to go with you."

Pollux raised an eyebrow, unimpressed by his story. Finally, he shook his head and smiled. "I think we'll need you, Cass. It'll take a few weeks for your body to heal, but after that I expect you to help man the oars. Can you do that?"

"I'll do anything," Cassius said. Pollux patted him on the shoulder and left the room with the rest of the group. Alone,

Cassius grinned and pumped a fist in the air. When the voyage reached Ithale, he'd find Kleos and end their war. Then Zinnon would see what he'd done and return his power.

For the first time in days, Cassius felt a spark of hope. Hope that he could right his wrongs. Hope that he could help these people, even in a small way. But most of all, the hope that he could take his throne with the gods once again.

ACT II

CRASHING WAKE

One dead for his past
Another for his future
The well is opened

Chapter Six

Deep within the bowels of *The Delphis*, Cassius worked his oar in a long room filled with the stench of sweat and the grunts of men at work. The third tier of the ship was the hottest and most undesirable of jobs. Only the most senior, experienced mates had the privilege of working at night when the temperatures were tolerable. If there were anything that could make the god of the seas hate sailing, it was this. The start of Kalokeri, the season of the sun, had only made the conditions more miserable. Additionally, Cassius' mood soured as he thought of the gods celebrating the new season together, playing games and enjoying themselves while he suffered.

Four weeks had passed since the voyage left Talasia, and it seemed they were no closer to their goal. Still, excited murmurs buzzed through the ship as they approached the port of Othenai, where they'd get to spend the day on land. Cassius intended to use the day to rest after a quick trip to the city's temple. If he'd learned anything about being a mortal, it's that soreness came as often as the wind. While he could adjust to his new face, Cassius didn't think he'd ever grow accustomed to the stiffness that plagued his muscles each morning. Others had noticed and even teased him for taking more breaks than the rest of them. Still, the soreness was better than the wounds he'd suffered during the storm all those weeks ago. It had taken two weeks of Pollux's care before Cassius could work. Something about that man and the way he carried himself made every burden seem lighter, more easy to carry. Cassius had seen it in the rest of the crew too. On the rare occasion that Pollux came to the bottom tier, the men and women worked with greater effort, as if reinvigorated by the captain's very presence.

"Hey, you," Damian, the servant of Kleos said as he jostled Cassius' shoulder. "I've been looking for you." He stepped over the bench and plopped down next to Cassius.

Cassius jumped at the sudden appearance of the boy, who he'd learned was only in his nineteenth cycle. Luckily, Damian and the others hadn't recognized him as a god in all their time together on the ship. To the mortals, he was Cass, a lowly farmer who'd never sailed before, but wanted to help after the destruction of their port. "Not a good time," He said through grit teeth as he pulled back on his oar.

"Switch spots with me."

"What? Why?"

Damian grabbed the oar from Cassius' raw hands and stepped over him. Using his foot, he nudged Cassius toward the middle of the bench. As if it were nothing, he began rowing the oar in perfect rhythm with the rest of the crew. "So," Damian said, "I think you need my help." Like everyone else on the ship, he wore a white chiton. Really the only difference in his appearance was the scar on his chin and the sword belted across his waist. As the newly appointed head of the ship's guard and only crewmate trained in the ways of war, Damian always kept a weapon close, even off duty as he was now.

"And why would I need that?" Cassius gave the answer dryly, secretly enjoying the break. He sat back and closed his eyes, settling into the feeling of his chest as it rose and fell with each breath. When his eyes opened again, he'd almost managed to forget the way the extreme heat seemed to warp the very air of the room.

With a click of his tongue, Damian looked Cassius up and down while maintaining the stride of his oar. "Cass, I really do hate to break it to you, but you're pathetic."

"Subtle."

"Well, I'm only honest." A couple of men behind them snorted at the comment, and Damian glanced over his shoulder with a grin. "Anyways, I can help you be less pathetic and more... I'm just going to say useful, but you know what I mean."

Cassius sighed and kneaded at an ache in his bicep. "Yes, unfortunately I do."

"What do you say? You in for it?"

"Damian, you haven't even told me what *it* is yet."

"Oh right." He chuckled and scratched his head with one hand, rowing the oar with the other. It was a feat Cassius could only dream of accomplishing. "I want to train you, to help you become stronger. Maybe you could even join the ship's guard." More snorts sounded from the crew. This time Damian shot them a harsher, more pointed look. "I'm serious," he said. "We could use the help and gods know you could too."

"Can't say I'll join the guard," Cassius said, "but I'd take the training. Anything to make this soreness go away. What do you want in return?"

A knowing smile stretched across Damian's face. "And in exchange, you'll teach me how to sail, right? More than just pushing an oar back and forth. I want to know how to really sail like they do on the upper decks." The comment was followed by several outright laughs from around the room along with a few snide comments about Cassius' poor skills.

"What makes you think I know how to do any of that?" Cassius glanced around, his palms suddenly sweating. He hadn't told anyone what he knew about operating a ship. In fact, it had been rather painful his first few days working when he'd had to listen to explanations about even the simplest tasks on the ship. If only these men knew that he'd been there when the first boats were built and the first sails hung, then he'd be up there on the higher levels with the real oarsmen. He could even be Pollux's first mate if that position weren't already held by Helena, who also served as the cartographer for *The Delphis*.

Damian drew in closer, reducing his voice to almost a whisper. "I saw you those first days on the deck watching the men work. I could see it in your eyes. Whoever you are, Cass, you aren't as lost as you pretend to be." His eyes darted from side to side. "Your secret is safe with me, but I really would appreciate the help."

Cassius' mind wandered to all the things he might teach Damian and he drifted away, reminded of other times he'd taught mortals the ways of seafaring. The thoughts only reminded him of that longing inside of his heart to regain his power and return to godhood. No matter how hard he tried over the past few weeks, the blockade Zinnon placed in the Union held strong, blocking him from his magic. More and more, Cassius was convinced that the only way to overcome his curse was to find Kleos and end the war he'd inadvertently started.

"Cass?" Damian's voice broke through the dreamy haze Cassius had fallen into.

"Oh," Cassius said, stumbling over an apology. After an awkward silence, he nodded his head and wiped the sweat from his hands on his chiton. "Why me though? Anyone else would be a better teacher than me."

Damian shook his head. "You're like me, Cass. You don't belong here."

"Oh, really? I hadn't noticed."

A grin stretched across Damian's face and he stuck out a hand. It was a gesture of goodwill amongst Kleos' followers. By reaching out his hand, Damian showed that he wasn't carrying a weapon. Cassius returned the gesture and they shook one another's hands. Truth be told, Cassius felt lighter having a chance to help the boy. It seemed a step toward mending the awful things he'd caused when he saved him from Kleos.

"That reminds me," Damian said, returning the oar to Cassius and standing at the front for the rest of the crew to see. "I bring news from Pollux. We'll reach port at midnight. After that, you are free to do as you wish. However, all those on cleaning duty are to complete their tasks before disembarking." A collective groan echoed through the room. "I know, I know. You should return to the ship by the time the sun sets tomorrow. If you don't make it on time, you'll be left in Othenai. Sounds good?"

A collective "aye" snaked its way through the rows of benches until all twenty seven of the men had agreed to the terms. Before ascending the ladder up to the deck on the side of the room, Damian turned to Cassius one last time. "Be ready. We'll start your training when you return to the ship tomorrow night."

By the time Damian had left, Cassius' thoughts had already begun to wander. He let the rocking of the ship take him away as he imagined what the other gods might have said about him when they met to celebrate the beginning of Kalokeri. Surely they mocked him. After all, none of them had ever fallen so far. He'd known all along that they were better than him. That's why the mortals worshiped them and not him. All along, he'd known it. It had haunted him ever since Antia had left him.

Drawing himself away from those thoughts, he shook his head, sweat falling into his eyes. It stung, but not more than the regret of who he'd been. Beneath his breath, Cassius made a promise to himself. "I won't be like that again," he said. "When I'm a god again, I'll serve them. I'll listen to Zinnon. There will be order." With the words, the sea seemed lighter beneath his oar, and a weight seemed to free itself from his shoulders.

Chapter Seven

The next day, Cassius stood alone at the edge of the main deck, resting his elbows on the railing as the blazing sun beat down on his back. The city state of Othenai stood before him, breaking up the monotonous plains that stretched out as far as the eye could see. In the center of the city stood a massive, open-air temple made up of a circle of eighteen marble pillars holding up a domed roof. The sky blue banner of Oura hung from the side, depicting the sun as it shined through a thin layer of fluffy white clouds.

"What are you waiting for?" Helena said as she pranced past, her dark hair braided behind her head. "We don't have all day." She rushed down the gangplank, leaping onto the dock and scaring away a couple of seagulls that perched nearby.

Cassius laughed and followed her down, though his legs were still too sore and heavy to make nearly the show out of it as she did. "What are your plans?" He said.

"You kidding?" She whipped around and smiled perfectly. "I'm here to figure you out, Cass. It's not everyday a man washes up after a storm."

Cassius ran a sweaty hand through his oily hair. "What?" Helena rolled her eyes and began walking down the pier. "I'm serious," he said as he caught up with her, wincing at the pain in his calves. "I'm just a farmer."

"A mysterious farmer," Helena said with a sense of awe. It didn't take long for them to reach the end of the dock. Othenai's port paled in comparison to Talasia's. Still, it served as a convenient spot to stop for rest and supplies on the journey to Ithale. "So, Cass, where are you taking me?"

Heat rose in his cheeks, and Cassius felt his ears turn a bright red. "I only wanted to go to the temple of Oura. After that, I was going to head back to the ship for some sleep."

"I didn't take you for a pious man, Cass." Helena rested a hand on his elbow for a second before pulling it away as they turned onto the main street. Ahead, the temple seemed to glow with a soft light, inviting him into its embrace. "You go on ahead. Get inside quick, a heatwave is setting in."

"How can you tell?"

She pointed to a puddle in the street that bubbled, steam rising from the surface. "I'll grab something to eat and meet you back here in an hour or so."

"You're not going to let me go back to the ship?" Cassius shifted from side to side, eyes darting this way and that. He couldn't help but feel like Helena had an ulterior motive. They'd only talked a few times before, and she'd never seemed so interested in him. Admittedly though, they'd only ever talked on the ship, where there was always work to be done.

Helena raised a dark eyebrow, a twinkle in her emerald eyes. "You really want to live your entire life on one of those tiny bunks?" As quickly as she said the words, she danced away, wandering down another street.

Despite the temperature, a chill ran down Cassius' spine. He didn't want to live any of his life on one of those bunks. He'd much rather be in his beachside hut in Talasia. As he walked towards the temple of Oura, he hoped that the goddess would be able to do something to help him. Part of him doubted that she'd be there anyways. As goddess of the skies, Oura had a tendency to run off on adventures of her own every once in a while. Still, the temple would be a good spot to rest while the heatwave faded.

Around the temple, the air shimmered with magic and cooled to a more pleasant temperature. Greenery grew around the stone path, budding with colorful flowers. People flocked into the bubble of cool air, using it as a refuge from the intense sun. It was said that the burns of a heatwave never faded with time or healing, cursing their victim for the rest of their lives. That was true. Except when a god chose to intercede and bless the burned with a healing.

Cassius stepped up onto the marble platform of the temple, where servants bustled about, burning prayers and preparing offerings. Each wore an outfit of unique style, nothing like the typical outfits of servants. Many wore pants or chitons cut so high that their thighs were visible—the type of clothes most gods would consider outright blasphemous. Not Oura, though. She had always made it a point to encourage individuality and freedom in her followers. It's what made her so popular among the mortals, a rarity for one of the deities of nature.

"Cassius?" Oura's voice said as she materialized out of thin air in a flash of blue light. Immediately as she appeared, Cassius felt the wind sucked from his chest. The air seemed lighter around him.

"Oura!" Cassius leapt forward into her arms. "You're here," he said, "you can help me, can't you?"

He met her stormy eyes and saw in them mourning and heartbreak. Oura pulled away. Cassius grasped at the fabric of her dress, but it slipped through his fingers.

"You'll help me, won't you?" Cassius paced back and forth, motioning with his hands as he said the words. "I can't be stuck like this. You don't know what it's like. Zinnon shouldn't have done this."

"Zinnon didn't do it." A pair of servants pulled over a plush leather sofa and Oura lowered herself into it, leisurely relaxing against the cushions but refusing to meet Cassius' eyes. A servant girl brought over a glass of violet wine, but Oura waved her away. "Sure, it was his idea, but we made the decision together."

The temple fell silent. It was as if all motion had stopped with the realization of what Cassius' siblings had done to him. They'd condemned him. And for what? To watch him suffer? Sure, he hadn't helped the mortals as much as they had, but that didn't warrant such drastic measures.

"I thought–" he began, but no more words would come. Sweat dripped from his palms, but he couldn't even find the strength to wipe it away. His chest tightened as darkness welled up inside of him, plaguing him with thoughts of his past failures. He remembered watching Mya on the beach, unable to hear her friends share stories and tell jokes. She seemed so alone, so separated from the rest of the group.

And Cassius could've saved her. At the festival, he could've given her the ability to hear. Honestly, it wouldn't have taken more than a snap of his fingers. Yet he hadn't. Despite all of his powers, he'd laid there helpless, unable to act. In that realization, he couldn't blame the gods for leaving him. Maybe they were right. Maybe Cassius wasn't meant to hold his power any longer.

Cassius' body sagged, and he hung his head low. With a light smile, Oura reached out to his essence and touched his soul, trying to share her love for him. He only ignored it and walked away, leaving the goddess and the temple behind. Even in his grief, Cassius found himself hoping that Oura would call out one last time and offer him the help he so desperately wanted.

. . .

Hours later, Cassius and Helena sat beneath the shade of a building constructed of fir wood, sharing a box of food together. The heatwave had settled and the familiar bustle of the streets had returned, but Cassius still felt a pit deep in his stomach after seeing Oura in the temple. He tried to distract himself by enjoying his time with Helena, but the sting of his failures nipped at his mind and encroached on every moment of silence.

"What is that?" He said, picking up a piece of brown meat by its edge.

Helena's jaw dropped. "You haven't had beef?" She grabbed the piece of meat and tore a piece free, popping it in her mouth and smearing some of the spices across her lip by accident.

Cassius' eyes widened. He'd never seen something so... disgusting. So disgusting in fact, that he only laughed and followed suit. Improper as it was, part of him felt freed of a weight he'd been carrying for a long time.

"You slob," Helena said, leaning over to grab a flask of water resting against Cassius' outstretched leg. As she reached for it, she turned to say something and Cassius realized how close her face was to his. He reached up a thumb to wipe the spices from her soft lips before Helena pulled away to sip from the flask.

"I guess I assumed sailors just ate fish all the time," he finally said, breaking the awkwardness between them.

"At sea, mostly," Helena said, pushing a rogue strand of hair behind her ear. "I get tired of it, honestly. A girl can only eat so much herring."

Cassius tilted his head. He'd never imagined that humans could eat for more than just survival. Now that he thought about it, the gods only ever ate the same foods at their festivals. Even as a mortal, he could practically taste the same old olives and goat meat that the gods had indulged in at the start of every season for as long as he could remember. He supposed that trying new things didn't really matter to the gods, for they had the eternities to do everything there was to do anyways.

"What?" Helena said.

"Nothing," Cassius said, "Just lost in a thought."

She raised an eyebrow before tossing him a chunk of amethyst purple bread. "Bet you haven't tried that either. It's made from a grain that only grows in the fields a day's ride north of here."

Cassius bit into the bread and immediately cringed. "It's so sour!"

With a laugh, Helena opened a can of honey. "Now this," she said, "is going to be the most fun I've had in a long time."

Chapter Eight

"Up!" Damian said, laying on the deck next to Cassius, silver moonlight shining on his face. Cassius grit his teeth, shaking as he tried to complete the push up. His arms quivered as he pressed his palms into the ground, sweat dripping from his hair. With a groan, he pushed himself off the deck until his elbows straightened. "Good!" Damian nudged his body. Cassius rolled to the side, lying on his back and staring up at the stars above. It was a windy night, which made up for the sweltering heat during the day. However, the wind blew opposite of the ship's course, so the ship had to keep its sails up to reduce drag.

"Look at that," Helena said from her stool a few spans away. "What'd that make, thirty-one?"

"Leagues better than where he was two weeks ago when we left Othenai."

Damian was right. Despite the time that had passed, the memory of his visit with Oura still kept him up every night. Training with Damian had returned some sense of purpose to his life. It also made rowing much less miserable. Still, having a mortal body turned out to require more maintenance than he'd ever imagined. Every morning felt like a battle to overcome the soreness in his joints and get out of bed.

"Alright, Cass," Damian said, leaping up to his feet and stretching out a hand. "No more sitting around. It's important to keep going when you're tired. That's the only way you get stronger."

Cassius grabbed his hand and stood up. He lunged to one side, stretching out his hip and thigh. "How many laps today?"

Damian only laughed and pulled something from a bag he'd set by the railing earlier. From it, he pulled a shortsword, sheathed in a black leather scabbard. "This is a xiphos." He handed it to Cassius in a reverent manner before resting a hand on the blade he kept on his hip at all times.

Of course, Cassius knew what it was called. He'd even used a xiphos before, but he'd never bothered to learn any of the techniques required to truly master the weapon. It was a short, double-edged blade, about the length of Cassius' forearm. After he tied the scabbard, Cassius reached a hand over to pull it free. A sharp pain stung in his hand as Damian swatted it away before he could grab the handle.

"What do you think you're doing?" Damian leaned on his back leg, tapping his front foot.

"We're training." Cassius furrowed his brow. "Don't you want me to be ready?"

"Never, and I mean *never*, unsheath your blade without knowing exactly what you'll do with it. It's bad practice. Only gods and tyrants carry around swords outside of their sheaths. For the first couple weeks of your training, we'll practice saying our purpose out loud before we unsheath. It's a good habit to get into."

"Seems like common sense to me," Helena said, meeting Cassius' eyes with a mischievous smile. She picked up her lyre from the deck and began strumming soft chords that drifted through the nighttime breeze.

"Now before we start, you have to know a couple things

about the practice of swordplay. Most teachers will teach one of only two strategies to fighting with a xiphos. The first is Stasi, also called the stance form." Damian squatted low and held his empty hands before him, one foot in front of the other. He showed the motions, waving his arm as if deflecting a strike then jabbing out at his invisible opponent. "It's about reacting to your opponent and timing your strikes with perfect precision," he said, returning to his center of mass. "My father taught me this at our home in Ithale in my eighth cycle. He was a great warrior, but a purist in the ways of this form. It didn't do him much good when Kleos' general challenged him to a duel of honor because he defied her orders."

"I'm sorry," Cassius said. "I'm sure he was a great man, worthy of the gods."

Damian shrugged. "He was set in his ways, and it led to his demise."

"So the second form is better?"

"I never said that." Damian dropped his stance, again pretending to hold his xiphos in his right hand. As he blocked attacks, he moved with the blade, dancing this way and that, taking a new form each time. Every shift, whether offensive or defensive, altered his position enough, making it impossible to predict his pattern. Behind him, Helena played an energetic tune on her lyre, matching the pace of his feet as they slid across the deck. "This," Damian said as he opened his eyes and stood straight, "is Choros."

"It looks better." Cassius laughed, eager to try it for himself.

"You're right." Damian chuckled under his breath and ran a hand through his dark hair. "If you want to be a master of the xiphos, you have to learn them both."

Cassius nodded. "So what happened to the general that killed your father?"

"That's a story for another time." Damian's eyes were

fixed on the horizon as he wiped a bead of sweat from his forehead. "Anyways, I found someone who would teach me Choros as soon as I could and began working my way up the ranks of Kleos' army."

"Is that how you ended up as Kleos' champion?"

"In a way." Damian bowed his head and took in a longing breath as Helena continued playing her lyre. A second later, Daedus, Mya's father, came stumbling out of his cabin at the back of the deck, carrying a bottle of mead and slurring something incomprehensible. Helena's song paused, and everyone on the deck seemed to turn towards the drunken man.

"Gods..." he said, tripping over his own foot and toppling over. Daedus tumbled into Cassius' arms, drooping over and mumbling to himself. The bottle in his hand dropped onto the deck and rolled away. The man looked up, his eyes glassy. "Mya," he said. "Where's Mya?"

For a second, Cassius thought Daedus saw right through him, seeing him for who he truly was–the monster who hadn't saved his daughter. Then a thin line of drool seeped from Daedus' lip and Cassius pulled away, letting the man slump over the railing. Damian held Daedus steady as he began to vomit over the edge. A woman stormed out from the cabin, wearing a white nightgown, hair frizzy from sleep.

"By the gods!" Daedus' wife and Mya's mother, Theora, said as she stepped up to the man. She had a hard face from years of providing for her family. "At some point I'm just going to give you to the crows!"

Another retch sounded and Pollux descended from the upper decks to see what all the fuss was about. When he saw Daedus, he rubbed his temple. "Where does he keep finding alcohol?" He spoke, more to himself than anyone else.

"Uh, Pollux." Damian scratched the back of his neck and looked down at his feet on the deck. "This one's on me."

"What?"

"Well, I didn't know you were trying to stop him from drinking so much. That much is obvious now." Damian forced a chuckle. "He said it helped him. I didn't think it would turn out like this."

With a groan, Pollux rubbed his sagging eyelids with his hand, making Cassius wonder how long he'd been without a good night of rest. "Don't do it again," he said. "And you're cleaning up whatever mess he makes. Now get him to bed and get Theora something nice to eat."

"Aye." Damian wrapped Daedus' arm over his shoulder and carried him off to the cabin. Helena offered her stool to Theora and began playing a new, somber tune on her lyre. As they waited, Pollux leaned back on one of the masts, whistling a melody to match Helena's song.

"Sorry about the boy. I should've told him not to let Daedus have anything," Pollux finally said to Theora at the end of his song.

She rolled her eyes and crossed her arms in her lap. "None of us really know what we're doing."

With a snort, Pollux stretched out his back and popped a couple knuckles. "You can say that again. Right, Cass?"

"I guess." He thumbed the pommel of his xiphos, trying to decide whether or not he should head to bed.

Above the group, a rope snapped and a man fell from the mast, slamming into the deck with a crash. One half of the rectangular mainsail tumbled down and the ship lurched with the sudden drag, turning a few degrees towards the side of the sail that had fallen. Already, *The Delphis* lost speed as wind blew against the course of the ship and caught on the sail. Pollux rushed to the sailor, who clutched his arm and cried out in pain. "Someone get that sail back up!" He said.

Without thinking, Cassius dashed to the mast, climbing up the pegs leading to the crossbeam where the mainsail attached. He scurried across, perfectly balanced as he pulled up the sail and tied it in place on the end that had come loose. The knot came easy, his fingers flying as they created loops and pulled the ends through. As quickly as it all began, it was over. For a moment, Cassius sat there, feet dangling over the edge as he basked in the light of the moon as it orbited the world. He closed his eyes, breathing in the salty scent of the ocean breeze. For the first time in weeks, Cassius felt a part of the seas. Still not a god, but at least one piece in the complex systems that he had created at Ktisis, the long forgotten creation of Pelagios.

He descended back down to the deck below, palms suddenly sweating as everyone stared at him, jaws hung. Even Theora, who barely knew him, had wide eyes. "And where did you learn to do *that*?" Pollux said, laughing and shaking his head. "Damian can't teach that."

Cassius blushed and stumbled over his words. "Um... farmers' school?"

Slapping her forehead with palm, Helena held back a guffaw. Pollux only rolled his eyes and stood. "One day I hope to hear the rest of your story, my friend. For now, consider yourself promoted. I want talent like yours on the main deck."

"I agree," Theora said, butting in on the conversation. "We need you if we're going to save my daughter."

Pollux shot her a dirty look. Just as he opened his mouth to say something to her, he paused and took a deep breath before turning back to Cassius. "I'm out a man for the night shift now." He looked down at the fallen sailor, who moaned in pain and held his elbow close to his chest. "His shift is all yours. Get used to sleeping during the day."

"I'm honored." Cassius bowed his head in respect to the captain.

"Helena," Pollux said, "Go tell the steering oarsmen to

take twenty strokes starboard. You think that's enough to get back on course?"

Setting down her lyre, Helena looked up at the stars, using her fingers to map certain sections. "Easily," she said after a few seconds. "I'll give the orders."

"Great." Pollux's eyes returned to Cassius. "You want to help me set this bone?"

With a gulp, Cassius knelt down beside the captain. The man panted, tears streaming down his face. "Gods help me," he whispered.

Pollux shushed him. "You don't need the gods now, I can help you. Straighten his arm, Cass." Cassius did as ordered, and the man shrieked. When Pollux put his hands on the arm to set the bone, the screaming stopped and a sudden peace came over the man. A sickening crunch ended the silence.

As the man was carried off, Cassius set to work, preoccupied by the events of tonight and, in particular, the way Pollux had stopped that man's screaming.

Chapter Nine

The *Delphis* rocked hard to the port side, and a sapphire wave crashed down from above, soaking Cassius. Rain pounded on the deck, and the low rumble of thunder echoed from the pewter clouds above. The sound of Pollux's commands drowned in the fury of the storm. Cassius held fast to a rope, wrestling against the mainsail and holding it strong against the gales.

The storm had caught them off guard, forming in the late afternoon during a powerful heatwave. Beside Cassius, a woman was thrown overboard where she'd been tying down some cargo. Another lurch of the ship in the opposite direction sent the crate sliding into Cassius, knocking him into the air. Just as he began to scream, his back slammed against the mast and he fell down onto his hands and knees.

Damian rushed to his side. "Are you okay?" he said, dark hair blowing in the wind.

Cassius pulled himself up to his feet and ran back to his rope, which flailed out of reach. If he didn't get it, the gusts of wind would rip the sails apart. "Help," he said, waving Damian over. Damian took a running start into a massive leap, snatching it out of the air and landing hard on the wet deck. As quickly as he could, Cassius grabbed it and pulled with all his strength against the mainsail.

"All strokes starboard!" Pollux said as he ran past toward

the steering oars at the front of the ship. He shouted it again and again until the ship began to turn, meeting the storm head on. The ship buckled beneath a wave, turning upright. When it seemed the ship would finally flip, a force seemed to push it in the opposite direction, slamming it down into its forward position.

Cassius took advantage of the brief peace, yanking the sail taut and tying it up on a metal loop built into the deck. Fighting against the wind, he ran to Pollux, who had taken to rowing one of the long steering oars at the bow. Rain slid down his face, his gaze transfixed on the horizon. The sea seemed to flee before his determination, breaking apart and weakening as he rowed with all his might. Below, Cassius could see the disordered mass of the other oars. While they were protected from the weather, rowing on seas as choppy as this was next to impossible, even for the most experienced. It required a tremendous amount of strength and dexterity.

"Pollux!" Cassius said above the sounds of the storm. "If we go too far west, we'll get stuck in the rock bays on the far side of Ithale."

"We won't survive any longer in this storm," the captain said. "We'll power through it and deal with whatever's on the other side later."

"Gods help us," Cassius said.

"No." Pollux finally looked back at Cassius, a scowl on his face. "The gods have forgotten us, my friend. I need you to count out fifty more strokes starboard then go down to the portside oarsmen and tell them to work with everything they've got. And tell Damian to get over here."

"I'm here, captain," Damian said, taking the other steering oar. Cassius ran to the stern, standing above the stairs down into the oars chambers on the portside. Beside him, a cabin door swung open and Helena walked out, steadying herself against the wall.

"Cass!" A sudden jerk of the ship threw Helena into his arms, almost causing him to lose count of oar strokes. "How did this start? I was only asleep for a few minutes."

He held up a hand to quiet her. When the oars chopped the water for the fiftieth time, he dropped down the steps into the oars chambers. "Full speed!" Before the men could say anything, he jumped down the ladder to the next tier, repeating himself. Finally, at the lowest tier, he took an oar of his own and began rowing with all the strength remaining in his mortal form.

The next morning, when the sky was bright and the ship had set down its anchor for the day, Cassius sat against the railing with Helena. Surrounding the ship were hundreds of white rocks jutting out of the water as far as the eye could see. The shadowy sliver of land that was Ithale painted the horizon. Cassius had apologized a thousand times for ignoring Helena during the storm, but if he hadn't hurried, the ship would've capsized in the very next surge of the storm's fury.

"I understand," she said. "You only did what was required of you. Who knows, maybe you saved us. So are you our mysterious hero now? "

Cassius blushed. "Anyone would've done it. I'm no hero. And I couldn't have done it on my own."

"Cass." She grabbed his hand and held it in hers. He hoped she didn't notice how sweaty his palms were. "I'm proud of you. That was a rough storm." Helena pulled her hand away, her eyes shying away with it.

"Thank you," he blushed. Ascending from the stairwell into the crew's quarters, Damian walked across the ship groggily and plopped down in front of them.

"Maybe I don't want to be a sailor," he said with a yawn.

Cassius laughed. "Storms like that are pretty rare. Well, depending on the season."

"Gods, you sure are smart for a farmer." Helena patted his knee, looking out at the sea.

"I wasn't a farmer," he said. It was a relief to finally have at least one of his lies off his chest.

Helena and Damian shared a look, then burst with laughter. "You think?" Damian said. "You know the seas as well as Pollux does, Cass. I don't think there's a single soul on this ship that still thinks you're a farmer."

As she stood up, Helena continued to chuckle to herself. "I'm going to go tell Pollux this. He won't believe it!" She took off towards the captain's cabin. Cassius scrambled behind, calling for her to stop. With a smile, she opened the door to the dark room, filled with nothing but a desk and a mattress where Pollux lay curled up and shirtless.

"Unless crows have descended from above to finish us off," Pollux said, eyes closed against the light shining from the doorway, "I don't wanna hear it."

"Actually–" Cassius began

"It's worse," Helena said in a grave tone. "You need to hear this immediately."

"Helena..." Cassius put his face in his hands, sighing to himself. Pollux cracked an eye as if to signal to his sister to continue.

"Cass told us something," she said. "You won't believe it. Turns out, he's not actually a farmer."

As he leaned his head back against his pillow, Pollux snorted and rolled his eyes. "Tell me something less obvious next time."

"I'm sorry about that." Cassius scratched his neck and felt the heat rise in his ears. "I didn't know what else to tell you."

"Cass, I really couldn't care where you're from as long as you keep sailing like you have these past couple days." Finally,

Pollux sat up and stretched out his back. "Now go wake up the day shift and tell them to get ready to start moving. We can get to Ithale by tomorrow morning if we stay on this path."

"What?" Helena said, stepping further into the room. "I thought we'd decided to take the long way around to avoid Kleos' navy."

"We'll avoid them this way too. Why waste an extra day backtracking?"

"Sure, but we'll have to maneuver through all of these rocks."

Pollux shrugged. "*The Delphis* can do it."

"I don't even have a full map of the rock bays."

"Make one as we go. You can sit with one of the lookouts." The captain stood and covered a yawn. He brushed past Cassius in the doorway and onto the main deck, pointing at the stripe of land in the distance. "That's our destination. We can make it there without a map, but Helena, if you make one, you'll be remembered for generations."

"Sailors never make it through the bays. It'll be impossible to turn around once we're too far in."

"She's right," Cassius said.

"I know. Which is why Kleos won't expect it. It's the most sure way to get Mya back."

"Do you want to get Mya back? Or do you want the glory of beating the odds?" Lip quivering, Helena stormed away, footsteps thumping into her cabin.

"Are you sure about this?" Cassius asked, the ship swaying beneath his feet.

"Aye." Pollux returned to his room and pulled on a button up white shirt. Cassius found it strange that the captain never wore the traditional chiton and himation, but he supposed everyone had their preferences. Pollux had never seemed the conforming type anyways.

"Then I'll go get the crew up." As he walked away, Cassius thought of returning to Kleos and ending the war. Hopefully, the gods would see what he'd done and return his powers. As much as he was coming to love the crew of *The Delphis*, every step felt harder than the last. Every day seemed to bring a new weight, and it all felt too much to carry. If anything, he'd learned that creating worlds was far easier than living in them.

"Everybody up!" Cassius said as he descended into the mushroom lit quarters of the ship. A few groans sounded. "Come on morning crew! It's time to get moving." Finally, people began to rise from their bunks. Within seconds, the crew bustled about and prepared to work. Cassius stopped by his own bunk and pulled open his trunk. It only contained a few extra chitons and the xiphos that Damian had given him.

After changing clothes, Cassius tied his xiphos around his waist and returned to the main deck as the ship began to move. He climbed his mast and let the sail down, securing it at the bottom crossbeam with a hitch. The knots came easily to his fingers even though he'd never actually learned them. They were as ingrained in his memory as his name. Once finished, Cassius leaned from the side of the mast and watched as Pollux instructed his superintendents on a maneuver. Making it through the rock bay would require slow, tedious movements.

A ringing pitch sounded, rising above the pipers' rhythms for all to hear. It grew into a chanting. Cassius' vision became blurry, and he slid down from the mast. He walked to the edge of the ship, gazing at the white rocks as they passed by.

"Cassius?" a voice said. He turned around.

Mya stood there, eyes filled with fear and blood running from her ears. "Cassius, please! Help me!"

Chapter Ten

"Help me!" The music screamed in his ears. Mya's form dissipated into mist, but the singing continued. Cassius dropped to the deck, holding his hands over his ears. The choir of voices drowned out all other thoughts. Shadows from the masts and sails grew in size, morphing into the forms of Oura and Phoebe.

"Lost child," they said in unison, their voices becoming a part of the song. "We made you human. We took your power."

"Stop it," Cassius said, crawling further up the deck towards the steering oars.

"You were weaker than the rest of us."

"Stop!"

Oura and Phoebe laughed and reappeared in front of him. "You failed, Cassius. Over and over again. You always failed, and you always will."

As he leapt to his feet, Cassius cried out and made a mad dash for the edge of the ship. Just as his feet left the ground to jump from the side, a hand grabbed the back of his chiton and slammed him back down into the deck. He groaned and rolled onto his side, clutching his rib as the singing voices faded away.

"Cass?" Pollux shook him again. "Snap out of it. We need you."

Cassius sat up, realizing for the first time that the ship had stopped moving again. The crew walked around in a daze, eyes glassy. The singing began again, though this time quieter and only in the back of his mind. Somehow, Pollux had managed to release its hold on Cassius. He rubbed his eyes and pulled himself up using the railing. Phosphoric yellow dots formed at the base of the jagged rocks. It wasn't hard for Cassius to identify them as siren barnacles. Hundreds of cycles ago, Cassius and Phoebe had made them. By releasing a special pheromone into the air, they lured in prey by causing hallucinations. Only they shouldn't be here. Cassius specifically engineered sirens to suit the colder, harsher waters around the edge of Pelagios. To survive in the Minean, they had either evolved thousands of cycles too early, or a god had altered their physiology.

A laugh burst from Cassius' mouth, and he hung his head low. Of course the gods had laid another trap for him. Somehow, they'd known he'd use this approach to Ithale all along. "You see those?" Cassius pointed out the barnacles growing on the sides of the rocks. "They're sirens. All of the men are going to feel their effects."

"And the women?"

"They'll be fine. Are there enough to run the oars?"

"Maybe one or two tiers.." Pollux grabbed a man and shook him out of his stupor. Like Cassius, the man came to his senses. Further down the deck, a splash could be heard as a man jumped off the deck. "We'll have to get these men back into the quarters. It's not safe for them up here."

"I don't get it. Why aren't you affected?" Cassius said. The two of them began to herd the men towards the quarters. Each time Pollux touched one of the men, they seemed to wake from their trance, though not as vividly as Cassius had. "And how are you doing that?"

"I don't know," he said, avoiding Cassius' eyes. Men began working their way up from the rowing tiers towards the edge of the ship. Cassius and Pollux rushed over, but four more dropped into the sea before anything could be done.

"What's happening?" Helena said.

"Sirens." Cassius held a man back from the railing. "Go tell all of the women. We'll need them to row the ship." With a nod, Helena ran off to help.

A man screamed from the upper deck. Cassius climbed the stairs to see Damian standing above a man, gore dripping from his xiphos. His eyes were dark and he winced as he stabbed the sailor two more times. "Damian!" Cassius held his hands up, keeping his distance. Damian began pacing around Cassius in a wide circle, his xiphos ready in his hand. Even though he knew Damian was better than him, Cassius drew his own xiphos. If anything, he could stall long enough for Pollux to come help.

"They took her," Damian said beneath his breath. In his words, Cassius could hear the sounds of the sirens louder in his own ears. He shook his head, trying to free himself from their song. The dead sailor's body transformed into Mya lying lifeless as blood trickled from her ears. Damian flew forward, jabbing at Cassius with his xiphos.

Cassius deflected the strike and slid one of his feet back, finding Stasi—the stance form. Before he could set it, Damian cut his cheek just above the corner of his lip. All Cassius managed to do was jab, forcing Damian to dance to the side and earning himself enough time to set the position.

"Mother?" Damian said, looking off to the side. Cassius tackled him, wrestling the xiphos from him. Pollux rushed up, glancing at the sailor Damian had killed with pity. He spoke nothing of it, lifting the spell and instructing Damian to go to the quarters. After helping Cassius up, they hurried back down to the main deck where a group of women stood at the side of the deck, pointing and gasping.

"What is it?" Pollux stepped up. Near the base of the rocks where the barnacles were, the sea began to bubble and churn. Steam rose into the air like the tentacles of a sea creature. Below, women began rowing the oars again. "Get below deck!" Pollux wiped a bead of sweat from his forehead as he gave the orders. The air grew hotter by the second.

"It's a heatwave," Cassius said, more to himself than anyone else. His chest began rising and falling rapidly. Between the sirens and the heat, they were going to die weren't they? He didn't want to die. All he wanted was to reach Kleos and end the war. A pit formed in his stomach as he looked to the bow of the ship. Ahead, a particularly massive rock jutted out of the water, blocking their path. "Do you see that?" He said, putting a hand on Pollux's shoulder.

"By the gods..." The captain ran up the deck and took up a steering oar. "Everybody take cover!" The sun burst alight, showering the world in golden rays that reflected off of the surface of the sea, blinding Cassius momentarily. When he closed his eyes, Cassius could see the silhouette of the gods holding Mya's lifeless body. A stabbing pain arced through his chest. He grit his teeth and took the other steering oar to help Pollux. In seconds, everyone else had vacated the deck. The oars slowed below as women told the others about the boulder in their path, but it was too late. If Cassius and Pollux couldn't steer the ship out of the way, their voyage would come to an end.

Together, they rowed. While Pollux pulled against the water on the portside, Cassius pushed on the starboard side. The ship turned a few degrees. Above, the sun washed the world in white light, and Cassius' skin prickled where exposed. Blisters already began to form on his neck and arms, and his rowing slowed as *The Delphis* approached the jagged stone. They'd managed to turn enough that the collision would not occur head on, but it still threatened to scrape across the entire starboard side of the ship.

"Move." Pollux shoved away and he fell down, the grainy deck hard against his burns. Cassius watched as Pollux thrust his hands into the air. A wave of blue energy crackled free from his palms, consuming the rock and dissolving it into emerald dust particles. By the time Cassius blinked, it was as if nothing had been there.

The sun grew in intensity once more, and his body felt alight with fire. His skin peeled, melting away from the light and radiating with heat of its own. Cassius screamed, his voice hoarse against the burning sun. The pain consumed him, overcoming even the voices of the sirens as fire seemed to tear through his insides. The smell of burnt flesh nauseated him. Blisters sizzled and hissed as they formed across his face.

Pollux knelt down, placing his hands on Cassius' chest. The last thing Cassius saw before closing his eyes was a fierceness in the way Pollux squinted against the light, lips pursed together as his curly hair fell past his shoulders. Eyes closed, Cassius whispered a prayer to Zinnon, begging one last time for the return of his power.

A drop of magic appeared in his soul. It increased, becoming a river that coursed through his veins and cooled his body, healing his wounds and sealing the spots where blisters had been. Cassius felt his body transform into his godly form and reached for the Union, only to find it was still blocked as it had been before. The source of this magic wasn't from the Union. Rather, it came directly from Pollux. His soul felt so much weaker than the gods, but somehow, Pollux managed to draw on the Union and use its power. Still, his jaw slackened and his eyes widened as he watched Cassius transform.

Cassius took hold of the magic and released a wave of energy, screaming as pain faded away from his body. The wave rushed from the ship, washing over the rocks and killing all of the siren barnacles. As he used up the magic, he transformed back into a mortal, tears streaming down his face as he lay there beneath Pollux's darkened gaze.

Chapter Eleven

The ship rocked and rocked for minutes on end while Cassius and Pollux sat against the railing under the shade of the mast. Cassius's burns had disappeared, and if anything he felt better than he had before. No one else had dared to come back up to the deck, and all rowing ceased below. If he listened closely, Cassius thought he could hear the whispers of people below, wondering if he and Pollux had survived.

"You're him," Pollux said. "You're Cassius."

"I am." Cassius stretched out his back, yearning again to feel the magic that Pollux had somehow given him. "And you can use magic. How long have you been able to do things like that?"

"Since the beginning of this cycle," he said. "It started a few days after Thriamvos began."

"Strange," Cassius said. That would have been around the same time Zinnon had taken his powers.

"Listen, Cassius." Pollux grabbed him by the wrist, forcing fierceness despite the obvious exhaustion in his droopy eyes and sagging shoulders. "I don't want anyone to know what I can do. Keep my secret safe, and I won't tell anyone yours."

Cassius nodded. "I thought you'd hate me for who I really am."

An awkward silence followed. "I do," Pollux finally said. "I hate all gods."

"Then why not get it over with and throw me overboard?"

"Because I'm desperate, Cassius." Pollux clenched his fists and slouched even further, burying his head in his hands. "People are counting on me, and I'm too small for any of this. No matter what everyone else on this ship seems to think, I can't do anything against Kleos in Ithale. I don't understand this magic at all. We're stuck in a rockbay in the middle of Kalokeri. I need you."

"You've seen me, though. I don't have my godhood anymore." A cool breeze blew past and Cassius sighed into it. "I can't help in the way you want me to."

Pollux stood, yawning and leaning out to watch seagulls fly on the horizon. Ithale wasn't any closer than it had been that morning. "Can you teach me how to use the magic?"

Cassius hesitated. Magic had always come naturally to the gods. Teaching it to a mortal would be like explaining how to think. "I'll try," Cassius said, unsure if he could live up to that promise.

"Then we'll face Kleos together, and I'll do whatever it takes to help you. If it means sailing to the edge of the world, I'll be there at your side." He reached out a hand and helped Cassius to his feet. Behind them, the door to Daedus and Theora's cabin creaked. They turned to see Theora stumble over Daedus' snoring body on the floor, a fiery blister covering the left side of her face. "Theora!" Pollux said, rushing forward to catch her.

She shrugged him away and lifted a weak finger to point at Cassius, ignoring the sunburn on her face. "It's him," Theora hissed. "He let them take my daughter." She pounced forward like a wildcat, reaching for Cassius with her teeth bared. Pollux held her back.

"I know, Theora," He said. She scratched at his arms, thrashing against his hold and cursing Cassius' name. Apparently, she'd been out during the heatwave and saw his transformation. After a few minutes, Theora began to pant and tears flowed unbidden from her eyes.

"Mya is gone because of him," she said, settling into Pollux's arms.

"Maybe, but he'll help us get her back too."

Cassius nodded and gulped. His palms began to sweat. "I promise."

"Your promises mean nothing." Her red eyes locked on him. "Pollux, we have to lock him up. We can use him as a bargaining chip with Kleos."

Cassius hung his head in shame. In many ways, she was right. Just as the gods had been right in punishing him. He did deserve this. His only real value might be as a bargaining chip.

"Cassius is not the enemy. I trust him, and I expect you to as well." Pollux closed his eyes and the muscles in his face tightened. Lines appeared on his forehead and at the creases of his eyes. The burn softened on her face, the color draining until it matched the olive tone of the rest of her skin. She winced as it happened, holding in a hesitant breath.

"I don't trust either of you." Theora pushed Pollux away and walked back into her cabin, slamming the door behind her as she stepped over Daedus' snoring body.

Pollux only watched before moving toward his cabin. "I need sleep," he said. "Tell the crew to make the ship orderly. We sail at sundown. You and Helena are in charge until then. After that, you can sleep in my cabin and I'll take the night shift." He looked over his shoulder one last time. "I'm trusting you. Don't mess it up."

Cassius nodded and turned to look out across the deck of

the ship. He took in a deep breath, set his jaw, and got to work.

Many hours later when the sun had set and the ship began to move again, Cassius lay in the bed in Pollux's cabin. It was much larger and softer than any in the crew's quarters. Still, he tossed and turned, unable to find sleep despite how tired he was. Outside, he could hear the deck crew shouting to one another as they managed the sails and steered the ship. The scent of cooked fish drifted up from the kitchens within the ship through a vent in the corner..

A shadow appeared in the corner, stretching until it covered the entirety of the wall closest to the door. A figure stepped out from the deepness of the shadow. The woman stood tall and wore a chiton that closely followed her body's curves. A forest green himation hung from one shoulder to the opposite hip. Phoebe, goddess of passion, tossed her hair over her shoulder as she took a seat at the foot of his bed. His soul could feel her essence, warm and familiar.

"Cassius," she said, resting a hand on his shin, "I've missed you."

He sat up, rubbing his eyes and sighing. "You put me here. At any point, you could have helped me."

"You're right. I did agree to give you this punishment. Partly as a lesson, but between me and you, I had other reasons as well."

"Phoebe, I'm not going to join whatever game it is that you've started this time. I'm going to help these people end their war with Kleos then regain my powers. Anything else is a distraction."

"Anything?" she said.

Cassius nodded.

"Even Helena? I've watched the way you look at her,

Cassius. You think she's beautiful." Phoebe chuckled, leaning in close. "You're falling in love again, brother," she said in whispered awe.

"Phoebe—"

"You have to understand, Cassius. I didn't agree to send you here to learn a lesson about order and godhood. You get to know what it is to truly live. Maybe the other gods wanted you to be punished, but I sent you here to experience something that I've always wanted." Phoebe glanced uncertainly down at her clasped hands. "Yes. Truth be told, I'm rather envious..." she spoke the last part so quietly Cassius nearly missed it.

"How shallow," Cassius said.

Phoebe's eyes darkened and she stood up, hands on her waist.

"You treat the humans as if they are perfect, as if every experience they have is some grand adventure. It's not. Most of these people don't want to be here. People are suffering here. Your envy completely disregards everything they've endured to be here."

The goddess raised an eyebrow and uncovered a lamp filled with fluorescent blue mushrooms that hung from the wall. Cassius squinted as his eyes adjusted to the light. Phoebe sighed. "Well, it seems you've learned something, at least."

"I... I think I have."

She shook her head. "It's a shame about the captain, though."

"Pollux? What about him?"

Phoebe rolled her eyes. "He's using our magic. He'll have to die for that, you know."

"Why?" Cassius stood from his bed and grabbed Phoebe's elbow. "He's learning things about magic that even gods don't understand. Phoebe, he's proving to us that the mortals can use magic. Think about the good that can be done by teaching them its ways. The crew needs him if they want any chance at facing Kleos. I need him if I want to get my powers back."

"It is not the natural order," Phoebe said, pulling her arm free from Cassius' grip. "The Union is a part of us. Humans cannot be allowed to draw from it. Think about the devastation that would occur if humans could all access it. Pollux is the start of a wildfire, and we must snuff it out before it becomes too dangerous to contain. It's for the protection of humanity, really. The order that must exist."

"I think you're wrong," Cassius said. He didn't have proof, but an echo from deep down told him that he was onto something. He only needed to push further, to take the next step towards understanding the magic. Pollux's use of magic seemed to stir something underneath Cassius's memories

"Phoebe, do you know what happened to our memories of the creation? What happened then that we cannot remember?"

Immediately, Phoebe spun away and walked back into the shadow. "Zinnon was right. You are lost, Cassius." She waved a hand and the air shimmered in the center of the room. The yellow sparks of light began to coalesce into a blob on the floor. As it grew, it sprouted eight jagged legs and a wooly abdomen. From one end sprouted a large thorax and the other a head with silver fangs. A single massive eye glowed deep crimson on the center of the head. For a moment, it sat lifeless as the drops of light poured into it. Finally, just as Phoebe disappeared completely, she breathed out a column of pinkish air. As that breath reached the beast, it shuddered, its lungs filling with air for the first time. It lifted itself up by its legs, stretching them out to either side. Now that it was standing, it was as tall as Cassius' waist and as wide as the bedframe behind him. It stepped about carefully at first before nuzzling its wooly head against Cassius' leg.

The door to the room swung open, and Helena stood in its frame with wide eyes and a mushroom lantern held in front of her. The one-eyed tarantula shrieked a hoarse, grating cry and charged.

Chapter Twelve

Cassius grabbed his sheathed xiphos from the floor of the cabin, chasing after the beast as it reared up on its back legs to attack Helena. Adrenaline shook his veins as he dove into the beast, tackling it just as it moved to strike. They tumbled over one another until the tarantula pinned down Cassius with two of its powerful legs. From beneath, it couldn't see Cassius with its one red eye. Somehow, Cassius had kept a hold of his xiphos, but without the movement of his arm it did him no good.

The crew began to scream as they saw the beast holding Cassius against the deck. It shrieked above their cries, raising its ovular head in the air and baring its silver fangs. Footsteps pounded across the deck and a blur slammed into the beast's side, pushing it off Cassius. Cassius quickly recognized the blur as Damian and used the moment to roll away and push himself back up to his feet. In the second it took Cassius to catch his breath, Damian became a whirlwind of slashes. He sliced at the beast's exoskeleton, but could not penetrate it.

"What is it?" Pollux said, running to Cassius' side.

"Cyclops." Cassius shuddered, remembering the stories of the beast. It was said to only be found in the deepness of the rainforests during Teras, the season of beasts. Cyclops fed on human souls, using them to create offspring.

"Can magic kill it?"

"Do you want the entire crew to see you use magic?"

"I want my crew to be safe." He shoved Cassius forward toward the fight. "Go help Damian."

In Cassius' defense, Damian had been doing fine so far. While he still hadn't managed to hurt the cyclops in any way, he batted away its long legs with precision, protecting himself from harm. As hard as Cassius tried, he could not remember how people had managed to break through the beast's armor. It seemed those memories were as lost to him as the memories of the world's creation.

His blood began to boil as he rushed into the fight, aiming for one of the joints between the monster's legs and abdomen. The cyclops sensed his approach, spinning wildly and releasing a spray of webs from its bulbous thorax. They drenched Cassius, distracting him long enough for the beast to leap out of the way. Only it made itself vulnerable for an attack from Damian. Damian recognized this, jabbed at its glowing red eye. The cyclops snapped his eyelid shut and Damian's xiphos bounced off. Only the tiniest of marks remained on the creature's dark eyelid as proof of Damian's strike.

A burst of wind blew in suddenly, lifting Cassius off of his feet and nearly throwing him off the edge of the ship. He managed to grab onto the cyclops, clutching the hairs of its back in his free hand. When the gale finally stopped, he looked up to see Pollux standing directly in front of the beast. He waved a hand and fire whipped from his palm, searing the cyclops across its maw. The air around him shimmered and crackled with magical energy. Pollux's dark hair blew behind his head as he seemed to pull magic out of the air, using it to blast the cyclops with all kinds of energy. The cyclops bucked back, sending Cassius tumbling down its back. After taking some of Pollux's shots, it released a two-toned dissonant cry into the night sky. Its eye opened again but had lost all of its glow.

The monster settled into a low position. Damian approached carefully from the side, signaling Cassius to do the same. Pollux breathed heavily, the color drained from his face. His breaths were heavy and his shoulders sagged. Just as Cassius and Damian came into the cyclop's reach, its eye burst with light. It reared up on its back legs, charging into Damian and pinning him against the mast. In that same moment, Pollux fainted and collapsed onto the deck.

Cassius stood there, watching as the cyclops held Damian's struggling limbs back. Its eye remained open, transfixed on Damian and batting away his strikes. It pressed one of its legs against Damian's throat and bared its silver fangs, hissing low against the whistle of the night's breeze. Cassius ran forward, ready to finish off the beast while it was distracted with Damian.

But before he could strike, he hesitated. What if he only made the creature more furious? What if he couldn't kill it and it attacked him next? Was it too late?

The cyclops yanked Damian's arm. A sickening crunch filled the air, followed by a howl of pain from Damian. The scream released Cassius from his panic. Leaping forward, he rammed his xiphos into the cyclops' eye. The sword pierced straight through the lens and viscous gel began to pour from the wound. He pulled his xiphos free, tossing it across the deck and grabbing the cyclops around its abdomen. As it screamed in pain, Cassius pulled it away from Damian, dragging it across the boat. With each step, the beast felt heavier. Finally, a couple of men joined Cassius as the cyclops breathed its last weak breaths. Together they hoisted it up and dropped it off of the side of *The Delphis*.

"Cass!" Helena sat above Damian, cradling his head in her lap.

"Don't move his arm." Cassius rushed back over. The ichor that had gushed from the tarantula's eye dripped from his clothing onto the deck. He knelt down, checking Damian's body for damages other than the broken arm. In several places, his skin had developed welts and bruises marked the attacks of the cyclops. Luckily, he'd survived, though the grimace on his face made his pain clear. "I don't know how to set the bone. We need Pollux."

Cassius turned around to see Daedus holding Pollux up by his arms while one of the crew members punched him across the face. Blood dribbled from his nose, and he seemed to have regained consciousness, though not for much good apparently. Theora stood to the side, sneering as tears fell from her eyes. Helena stormed over, footsteps pounding against the deck.

"What are you doing?" she shouted, voice pointed as she pulled the crew member away. She looked to Daedus, who for once lacked his drunken slurs and imbalance.

"Didn't you see?" Daedus shoved Pollux to the ground and placed a foot on his back. "He's been hiding among us the whole time. He's one of the gods."

"No." Cassius stepped forward, grabbing Daedus by the arm. "He's not. It's just magic."

Daedus raised his other hand as if to hit Cassius when Helena pulled Cassius away. "Don't let him hurt you too," she said, keeping him close to her.

For a moment, they all stood there awkwardly while the crew surrounded them. Cassius stared down Daedus, unsure of what he should do. Theora had seen him transform into a god when Pollux had healed him. She knew who he was, but did she actually think Pollux was a god too?

"Take Cass too," Theora finally spoke. Her voice cracked as a tear ran down her face, all but confirming Cassius' fears.

"I saw them together during the sirens. They're both gods. They're using us."

"Cass?" Helena said.

Cassius moved forward. "You can't do this, Theora. We stopped the sirens for Mya. We weathered storms for her." He jabbed a finger into her chest. "Whatever you think about us, it's wrong. We want to save Mya just as much as you do."

She met his eyes with a look of hatred so genuine that he knew in that moment that she truly saw him as a liar. To her, Cassius had rejected her broken daughter. He had snuck onto *The Delphis* and for all she knew, Pollux and Cassius were leading the crew into a trap.

"It's obvious, isn't it?" she said, speaking more to the crew than Cassius. "Cass shows up out of nowhere with a deadly wound and pretends to be a farmer. Then a sailor just so happens to fall and hurt himself so Cass can be promoted." As she spoke voice became dryer and more pointed, losing the weakness it had shown only seconds ago. Theora had been waiting to expose him for a long time and now she had Pollux in her grasp as well. "They used the storm to drive us into the sirens. And now, a monster appears from the cabin where Cassius was asleep and Damian, our only chance of an audience with Kleos, is in danger. Don't you see it? The gods war with us."

A murmur snaked through the growing crowd as the crew whispered amongst each other. Theora played it to her advantage, giving the crew time to understand her accusation. Helena huffed and straightened her posture. She let go of Cassius' arm and rested a hand on another woman's shoulder. He needed her to persuade them. Theora had ensured that the crew would never trust his word again.

"She's right," Helena said. "This voyage has been awful in many ways. We've endured so much and come so far, but it seems that the stars have lost their shine and the crows are beginning to descend from above. That is not what Pollux stands for. It is not who Cass is. When the ship bent before the storm, they stood against it. We must not turn what could become legend into tragedy by giving up when we are so close to saving Mya."

Theora clicked her tongue, rubbing a dried tear from her face before pursing her lips and narrowing her eyes. "Take them to the hold. I will talk to Helena personally and convince her of the lies these men have forged for us."

Cassius objected and tried to get closer to Theora. The group surged forward, swallowing him in their mass. A fist swung, slamming into the side of his head and knocking him out cold.

Chapter Thirteen

"Right under my nose," Pollux said from his spot lying on the floor, tossing a fluorescent green mushroom into the air and catching it. He'd been doing it since Cassius woke up an hour or two ago with a splitting pain in his head and several cuts and bruises that hadn't been there before he'd passed out. Pollux sighed and threw the mushroom again. "Mutiny. That's a first for me."

"Not me."

"No?"

"Well, to be fair. The other times I was on the other side of it."

"You?" Pollux laughed as the mushroom hit the wooden ceiling of the hold and dropped down into his palm. "I don't really take you for the rebellious type."

"Why's that?" Cassius leaned back against the curved wall. The ship rocked less beneath the cargo hold, where Cassius and Pollux had been locked up by Theora and her mob.

"You're too easy to get along with."

"And is that supposed to be a bad thing?"

"Depends how you take it." Pollux sat up and threw the mushroom to Cassius this time. Cassius caught it and tilted his head. What did Pollux want him to do with it now? "It's called catch, God of the Seas. You throw it back," Pollux said, rolling his eyes. "And what I meant is you don't try very hard to separate yourself. You just flow with the current. Which seems fitting enough."

Cassius tossed the mushroom back to Pollux. "I guess," he said. It felt strange to be talking to a mortal about himself. For so long now he'd tried to be so careful not to expose his divinity, and now everyone had figured it out. Surely on the upper decks Theora and Daedus were telling everyone of his failures at the festival. Anytime now the crew would march down here and finally kill him. Still, Cassius worried more about Helena than himself. Had they hurt her? Worse, did she hate him as Theora and Daedus did?

Between throws, Pollux chuckled to himself. He rubbed his brow. "I can't believe you participated in a mutiny. You've always been so... obedient."

Cassius snorted. "You should ask Zinnon about that. The last thing he'd call me is obedient. Order is the only thing that matters to him. And the seas are anything but order."

"Is that why you're here?"

"It is," Cassius said. "The last words he told me were that I'd forgotten what it means to be a god. He said that gods are responsible for maintaining the order of humans by seeing to their needs and guiding their paths."

Footsteps pounded above and the two of them fell silent. Cassius glanced down, preparing for the trapdoor in the ceiling to open and for their demise to drop into the room. He wondered who Theora would send. Damian would be up for the task if he weren't hurt. Surely, he hated Cassius for nearly getting him killed at the festival in Hestia. The footsteps faded back to the higher levels of the ship and Cassius and Pollux released the breaths they'd been holding.

"The mutiny was seventy or eighty cycles ago now. Long before you were born," Cassius said. "It was on a merchant vessel, much smaller than this one. One of the oarsmen was named Lantos. He worked hard and helped the ship in many ways, but he was also odd. No matter how hard he tried, Lantos always stood apart, too awkward or scared to try to interact with the rest of the crew. While they drank or sang songs, he'd watch the waves, covering his ears with his hands to block out their noises. The crew decided that he was disturbed in some way, but still always kept an eye out for him to make certain he was safe." Cassius paused and tossed the mushroom over to Pollux. They continued tossing it back and forth, but Pollux kept quiet, intent on taking in the story.

"One night, during a storm, Lantos had a fit of panic. In his fear, he screamed and howled. None of the crew was able to sleep, including the ship's captain. He knew if his crew couldn't sleep, they wouldn't be able to work their hardest. So he beat Lantos until he could no longer cry. Granted, it did help most of the crew sleep. Several men spent the rest of the night trying to fix Lantos up. Now matter how hard they tried to help, Lantos did not seem to respond to their care. He was lost in his guilt. For all he understood, he deserved the beating. Eventually, those taking care of him exhausted all their efforts. When they woke up in the morning, Lantos was gone. In his guilt, he'd leapt off the ship and drowned in the sea."

Silence filled the room and Pollux held the glowing mushroom close to his heart as they listened to the waves outside. In the familiar rhythm of their rising and falling, Cassius remembered that day as if it were only a season ago. "Lantos prayed to me before he died. He said, 'Lord Cassius, let me die in peace. Do not save me.' It broke my heart, but I tried to make it as easy as possible for him. I softened the seas and let them take him quickly and without suffering. Later that day, while the captain wasn't paying attention, I appeared to the crew. They were already making their plan, but my help made it easy. We locked the captain away, much like you and I are now. I led the ship the rest of the way. At its destination, we set the captain free but did not allow him to stay aboard. After that, I left and never saw or heard of them again."

Pollux bowed his head reverently for a moment. "I understand the captain," he said, the confession soft on his lips. "More than I'd like to admit. Partly because I know what it takes to run a ship. A disruption like Lantos' night terrors really would be hard to manage."

"You're right."

"But treating another human like that... It's unforgivable." Pollux leaned forward, tapping a finger on the floor. "My grandmother used to tell me that every person's life is worth more than a thousand sunsets."

"She sounds like a wise woman."

Pollux smiled. "When she was young, she was blind. Every day, she would sit on the beach to enjoy the scent of the sunset's breeze."

A chill ran up Cassius' spine as he realized that he knew Pollux's mother. In fact, he'd been in love with her.

"A god gave her the gift of sight. She never said who or why, but her gratitude showed every day in the way she used her gift." Pollux leaned his head back and closed his eyes.

"What was her name?" Cassius said, the words forced from his throat.

"Her name?" He cracked an eye. "Antia. Why?"

"I..." Cassius choked up. "It was me, Pollux. I healed her. I was in love with her, and I wanted her to love me back. When she chose your grandfather instead, that's–"

"That's when you stopped blessing mortals."

Cassius nodded. "Did you know?"

"No. I wasn't lying when I said she never told me the story." Pollux stood up and joined Cassius on the other side of the hold. "I'm sorry, Cass. You know I distrust the gods, but a broken heart is a form of suffering I would not wish on my worst enemy."

Cassius shrugged. "It's over now. Mortals hate me. The gods hate me. There's nothing left to do about it anymore."

"What? How can you say that?"

"How can you not? We're only delaying the inevitable now. Pollux, mortal lives are short and Theora just made ours even more so."

Pollux bellowed a bold, genuine laugh. He wiped a tear from his eye and the tension eased in his shoulders. "You really don't understand mortality at all. Sure, things don't look too great for us, but we've got a long way to go till Theora gets her way. Don't dig your grave too early, my friend."

"You don't think the crew has turned against us?"

"Oh, no. Maybe some of them, but I'd bet Helena's hard at work planning to get us out of here. She's a better sister than I deserve. Besides, I've got this magic, and I'm finally feeling up to using it again."

"Right," Cassius said, surprised at how determined Pollux seemed. He'd always assumed that mortals were fragile, but in many ways, Pollux was stronger than many of the gods. "When I used magic, it was like reaching into a well within my soul. I drew it out and used it to shape the world around me. It felt different when you healed me. Rather than a well from inside, it felt like a bucket of water being poured into me."

Pollux nodded, his face becoming stoic again. "It's different for me. I draw the magic from my surroundings. It's in everything. The wind, the stars, the crew. The universe itself holds all of the magic, I just have to take it."

"Strange," Cassius said. He scratched an itch on his neck and considered what Pollux had said. "It started recently, right? You told me that you used it the first time at the start of Thriamvos."

"A couple of days after, actually."

"That's right," Cassius said. Pausing to consider the timing and the coincidence.

"That's right at the same time when I became a mortal. Pollux, what if I'm what was stopping you from using the magic before then? What if it wasn't just me, but if all gods are stopping mortals from using magic?"

"How?"

"I'm not sure. You said that you take magic from the world around you. The gods, though, pull magic from inside themselves. What if we hoard the magic? Pulling into ourselves so that only we can use it? "

Cassius froze as he felt whispers of truth unlocked deep inside his memory. The sudden realization temporarily took his breath away.

"The gods turned me into a mortal by taking away my magic. You used that magic once it was free of me. Wouldn't that mean that all gods are just mortals with magic?"

"It could, but it seems impossible that such a thin line separates mortals from god.."

"I don't know," said Cassius. "I need to talk to Zinnon. There's so much I want to know now that I've experienced mortality and seen you use magic. Before becoming a mortal, I thought I knew so much. It's becoming so much clearer to me that I don't."

"If gods are storing all of the magic, then they have to stop," Pollux said. "We need to be able to access it for ourselves. It's a tool, Cassius. It could make mortal lives better in so many ways. We could live for ourselves, no longer captive to the whims and mercies of the gods"

"I agree." Cassius rubbed a hand across his tired eyes. "You're right, but I have to see the other gods. They have to know this."

Pollux tossed the mushroom into the air and caught it in his other hand. "Let's start with getting out of the hold." He stood up and pushed on the trapdoor. It swung open without any resistance. A crewmember peered down into the hold, eyes wide and a spear in his hand. "Listen," Pollux said. "I helped design this ship, so I know there's no lock here. It's not made for prisoners. We would've heard if you'd dragged something over it too." He reached a hand up to the crewmember. "You can either stab me or help me, it's your choice."

Chapter Fourteen

Bright daylight greeted Cassius and Pollux as they climbed the steps out of the ship's storage hold. The crew of the ship bustled about, preparing to dock in the port of Ithale. One of Kleos' ships drifted close by off the starboard side, but allowed *The Delphis* to move into the city unharmed.

The city of Ithale was built on a stony cliff. Jagged rocks and wooden beams supported massive platforms covered in tent-like houses and shops. Colorful banners hung over the sea, streaming in the wind. Most prominent of all was the fortress sitting on top of the mountain. Polybolos, massive mounted bows, swiveled toward *The Delphis*, ready to fire in the event of an attack. Behind the fortress on the summit of the mountain was the temple of Kleos. Surely, that's where Mya would be.

"They've got Helena in your cabin, Pollux," Damian said as he stepped out from a shadow. He still kept his xiphos tied to his side, though his arm was wrapped tightly against his chest at an awkward angle. Like Cassius and Pollux, his skin swelled in many places from the fight with the cyclops. "Daedus and Theora struck a deal with Kleos. They're going to turn the two of you over in exchange for Mya."

"Great," Pollux deadpanned. "What do we do, Cass?"

"We can't fight here. Kleos will overwhelm us before we

can take back control of *The Delphis*." Cassius scratched his head. "What if we let them turn us over? They can get Mya, then you and I will escape Ithale together."

A group of crewmen stormed over, spears held high as they shouted for Cassius and Pollux to stop. Pollux moved to fight, but Damian held up a hand. "They're compliant," he said, his voice dry and tired. "Tie them up and get ready to hand them to Kleos when we dock."

The soldiers looked up just as Theora descended the steps from the upper deck. "Under whose orders?" She said, eyes locked on Cassius.

"Daedus," Damian lied. "Believe it or not, he's eager to have his daughter back." He shoved Cassius forward and onto the floor. Cassius played along, trying to resist momentarily before letting himself collapse. A few seconds later, Pollux joined him on the deck. The guards returned with a length of rope, pulling Cassius up and tying him against the front mast so all of Ithale could see him. They tied Pollux up on the railing a few paces away. The soldiers on the ship escorting *The Delphis* into port cheered and roared. Cassius could almost smell the wine on their breath, even from so far away.

"Cassius," Daedus said, stepping up from behind him, "have you come to regret what you've done?"

"Who were you again?" Cassius said in a drawl.

Daedus' face reddened and he placed a hand on Cassius' throat. "I'm not a soldier. I'm not a sailor. I don't belong here."

"I noticed."

"I'm on this voyage because I love my daughter. You will never know how to love, god of the seas." He huffed and stormed away, yelling at a sailor. The ship slowed as the steering oarsmen at the hull did most of the work to guide it into port. A small army of hoplites stood on the dock, armed to the teeth with spears and xiphos. Damian came to the front of the ship to untie Cassius with his one good hand as they shouted his name, calling him out as a coward and a traitor.

"Don't let them get to you," Cassius said underneath his breath. "You're a good man. When all is said and done, I'd like to have you by my side while I rebuild Talasia."

Damian nodded, unusually quiet. Whether he said it or not, he felt the sting of the hoplite's words. At one point, these had been his people. He'd proved himself to them. Now they wanted to kill him because of Kleos' pride. "Pollux healed my arm. I'm going to keep it hidden for now," he said. "I know several people on board will help me take back the ship. Once we're away from Kleos' navy, we'll set Helena free and be ready for the two of you to come back, however you plan on doing that."

"Hopefully I'll be a god," Cassius said. "That would make it easy."

Damian pulled free Cassius' bands just as the gangplank set down on the docks. Ahead, Daedus held Pollux's arms behind his back. They walked down the gangplank where the captain of the hoplite army stood. Mya stood at his side, holding his hand and looking around with curiosity. She wore a white chiton and her hair was braided behind her head. Her face was soft and clear. Upon seeing her, Daedus let go of Pollux and rushed over. A hoplite stepped between them, smacking Daedus' knee with the butt of his spear.

"You'll have her when we have the god," the captain said. Mya pulled her hand free from the captain's side and began signing to her father, her eyes filled with worry. The captain grabbed the back of her dress and held her away. "Is this him?"

"Yes." Damian shoved Cassius onto his knees. Cassius played along, keeping his head hung low.

"And this is the heretic?"

Pollux fell down beside Cassius. "He is. Lord Kleos will be proud of you," Damian said. "Now hand over the girl and we'll be off."

"Oh," the captain said, "the girl's parents must not have told you."

"Told me what?"

Cassius looked up as a group of hoplites charged, throwing Damian on the ground. Against so many of them, his attempts to fight back were useless. He didn't even have time to draw his xiphos. A pair of hoplites dragged him between Pollux and Cassius. The three of them knelt on their hands and knees, shoulders pressed against one another.

"You kept your end of the bargain. Now it's our turn." The captain pushed the girl to her father. Daedus embraced her and picked her up, rushing up the gangplank onto *The Delphis*. The captain of the hoplites knelt down, holding up Damian's head by the chin. "You were the best of us," he said. "When did you lose your glory?"

Damian spit in the man's face. "I've seen monsters," he said, "and I've seen maelstroms. Kleos sent me to battle more times than I can remember. I did everything for him." As the crowd of soldiers pressed in to hear him, Damian held his head up high into the air, his voice strong despite the surrounding enemies. "There is more than glory, brothers. Violence has made us strong, but only peace can make us eternal. I am done being a breaker. It is time for me to be a hero, to build something everlasting."

The captain held up a hand to quiet the army. "You have disgraced us, Damian." The captain grabbed Damian by the hair on the back of his head.

Damian grabbed the man's braced forearm. "Please," Damian said, "there must be a way to find peace."

"There is. For Denara, at least." With that, the captain grabbed a spear from a nearby hoplite and rammed it through

Damian's eye with enough force that a crack formed up its shaft. The world seemed to fall silent for a moment as Damian raised a hand to the eye, feeling the blood dripping down from where the spear protruded. His body began to tremble as he lost control of the muscles in one side of his face and his cheek and eyelid began to sag. Pollux reached out a hand to heal him when a red light shot from the crowd, enveloping Damian's body and turning it to dust.

"Cassius!" Kleos bellowed as the crowd parted. His crimson cape billowed behind him as he clutched a xiphos in his hand. Cassius remembered what Damian had told him weeks ago when training with the xiphos for the first time. Only gods and tyrants walk around with their blades unsheathed. Kleos, it seemed, was both. As he laid eyes on Cassius, the corners of his mouth turned upward in a wicked grin. "Nice of you to join us, brother" Kleos snarled as he motioned for two of his hoplites to grab the prisoners and follow him. "The gods are waiting for us in my temple. They're here to put you down once and for all."

Chapter Fifteen

Cassius' soul felt exhausted of strength as the hoplites dragged him off of the wooden lift that had brought them to the top of the cliff. A pulley system of stone weights and counterbalances operated the lift, a feat of engineering that impressed even Zinnon. Now, as Kleos marched ahead of the group, the only thing that separated Cassius from the entrance to the temple was a set of onyx stairs. Inside, Cassius felt the urge to let go of everything, to allow himself to fade away into the universe and forget all he'd ever known. The hoplites pulled his body up step by step. Next to them, Pollux walked on his own, his hands tied behind him and an expression of defiance lingering on his face.

Kleos pushed open the grand stone doors to his temple. Inside the gods stood in a ring, conversing amongst one another while they ate olives and drank wine. Zinnon stood in all white at the back of the room. Once he saw Cassius, he held a hand up to call the gods attention. "My lost child," he said, each step faster than the last as he hurried to Cassius. The hoplites handed Cassius to Zinnon. The god embraced him, holding him in his strong arms. "Oh, Cassius," Zinnon said. "It has been too long."

Cassius slumped in Zinnon's arms. The weeks of being a

mortal pressed their weight on him. After all he'd been through, he felt so tired and worn.

"He is weak now, Zinnon," Kleos said as he moved across the room. He took a seat in his onyx throne at the center of the room. "It is exactly as I predicted."

"You underestimate him. He has learned much." Zinnon tried to heal Cassius, but his body would not accept it. He wanted—no, needed—his misery to end. He'd decided on the journey up the mountain that everyone was right about him.

He was not good enough to be a god. He was not strong enough to be a mortal.

"And what of the mortal?" Phoebe said, stepping forward in the arc of gods. "His magic is a danger to humankind."

Zinnon and Phoebe shared a silent, knowing look. Zinnon helped Cassius to stand on his own before scratching his chin. "You all do not remember it," Zinnon said to the gods, "but when we created the world, we harnessed the magical current of the universe to create Pelagios. We created order from nothing. In the early days, we gifted mortals the same access to magic that we had, just as Pollux has now."

Zinnon looked down on Pollux, pausing as if deciding what to say next. Finally, he spoke. "They used the power of creation to commit atrocities. Those were the most violent, bloodthirsty days of humankind's existence. It is why we stepped in and stopped them. It is why mortals cannot be allowed access to magic. It is why we must provide order."

Cassius looked down at the floor, staring at the reflection of his mortal form. Over the past several weeks, he'd grown accustomed to imperfection. He'd learned to live with the pimples on his face and the looseness of his skin against his muscles. Only now, in front of the rest of the gods, it only reminded him of how much he'd failed. First, he'd failed as a god to help those who needed him. Now he'd embarrassed himself as a mortal, proving that he was incapable of accomplishing anything at all. Everytime he tried to do good, he ruined everything even more.

"No," a voice spoke. It was small, but steady and defiant. Pollux stepped forward, untying his hands with magic. "You're wrong." He looked so fragile in the face of so many gods. Their perfection dwarfed him, but he stood strong. "You've taken our freedom. Our choice. We need the magic. There is so much good that can be done, and I've proven it. You haven't seen me murder or destroy with this gift. No, I've used it to heal and to protect."

Phoebe scoffed, throwing her perfect hair over her shoulders. Golden magic rushed out from her form, surrounding Pollux and lifting him into the air. He used his hands to summon magic of his own, vanquishing her power and dropping to the floor in a crouched position. "You must see," he said. "Magic is a tool, and tools will always have the potential to be misused. Whether it's by a god or a mortal, there will always be a way for magic to be destructive. By taking it from mortals, you aren't protecting us. You're limiting our ability to learn this for ourselves. We can use the magic for good, but not unless you give us the chance."

Zinnon put a hand on Phoebe's shoulder to stop her from lashing out at Pollux again. He looked to Cassius next. Cassius did everything he could to avoid meeting Zinnon's golden eyes. Eventually, all of the gods were staring at him. "Is this what you have learned, Cassius?" Zinnon said.

Cassius' hands sweat and his throat dried. "Yes," Cassius said. "We're binding up the magic so they can't use it. But Pollux deserves the power more than I do."

Several of the gods rolled their eyes, but Zinnon only pursed his lips. Pollux walked over to Cassius, taking his side as Phoebe watched him with a careful gaze. "Are you okay?" Pollux said beneath his breath. Cassius only looked down at the polished floor. He needed this to be over.

"Zinnon," Kleos said from his onyx throne, "the battle is beginning."

"Battle?" Pollux said, voice drowned by the growing excitement of the gods.

"Go. Begin watching. I will finish speaking to Cassius and Pollux then join you." Zinnon waved a hand and the gods began leaving the temple, staring at Cassius and whispering as they left. Kleos and Perseo found each other and began arguing about whose ships were faster. They exchanged some coins, and Cassius realized they were taking bets on who would sink *The Delphis*.

Once everyone had left and the doors to the temple shut behind them, Zinnon began pacing back and forth, running his hands through his curly white beard. "Cassius, you have not learned as much as I'd hoped."

"Don't do this," Pollux said. He stepped up to Zinnon and jabbed a finger in his chest. "Can't you see what he's been through? He's struggled more than any of you ever had to."

"Stay out of this, mortal." Zinnon blew a puff of air at Pollux that sent him tumbling back until he hit one of the room's walls. "Cassius, you must accept these things. These are the ways of the gods. It is how the world must be if humanity is to survive."

"No, it's not," Cassius said. Pollux stood up, eyes locked on Zinnon. He stormed over, eyes glowing white as he drew on more magic than he ever had before. When he reached Zinnon, he grabbed him by the collar of his chiton and lifted him into the air despite his massive size. For the first time that Cassius could remember, Zinnon's eyes had lost their usual stoicism. His entire face sagged with fear as he tried to pry Pollux's hands off of him.

"You are afraid," Pollux said. "Not that we will destroy ourselves, but that we will destroy you. That if we can use the magic, we won't need your help anymore. You're afraid of being irrelevant." Pollux shook Zinnon, his teeth grit and his eyes burning. The air shimmered around him, blurring slightly. "I am living proof. Proof that magic is made for mortals. Proof that the gods' job is finished." He threw Zinnon across the room, where he smashed into one of the black pillars. A section of the ceiling crumbled and cracked, but the structure itself held strong. For a split second, Zinnon's form vanished in a puff of orange smoke. Then the smoke coalesced back into Zinnon's body, and he raised his hands in front of him, summoning red chains from the air that bound Pollux, preventing him from fighting back any further.

"Choose," Zinnon said, panting heavily as he concentrated on stopping Pollux. "You've seen now what magic is capable of. Now you must choose. Save yourself or save Pollux."

The barrier blocking Cassius' soul from the Union dropped, and Cassius felt the power there again, waiting for him to take it for himself. It could be his. He could be a god again, but choosing his power meant that Pollux would die. Or he could live the rest of his days as a mortal, and Pollux would live.

As much as he wanted Pollux to live, he was so tired. He couldn't keep fighting each day to be alive. Mortality had taken too much of his strength.

"Do it," Cassius said, tapping the Union inside of him, letting it transform him back into a god. His muscles swelled to their natural physique and he grew taller once more. As he became a god again, he begged the magic to take away his pain, to make him whole again. It didn't.

As Cassius grew, the chains constricted around Pollux, strangling out his mortality even as magic filled Cassius once again with his immortality. Finally, both the chains and Pollux vanished into nothingness.

"Good," Zinnon said, a look of satisfaction on his face. "Order is restored."

Without a word, Zinnon strode out of the room and to the cliffside. Cassius remained where he was, observing the wreckage of the pillar where Pollux had thrown Zinnon. Just like Damian, Pollux died. Cassius let them both die. Alone in the temple, Cassius fell to his knees, a heavy tear falling from his eye. They were dead, and it was his fault.

Cassius summoned his powers, transporting himself onto the deck of the Delphis. Chaos surrounded him as the crew bustled about, drawing the sails and manning the oars. On the upper deck, Helena shouted orders and commanded the crew. Two of Kleos' ships sunk behind *The Delphis*. Apparently, Helena had managed to put up a fight. Despite her efforts, the combined might of Kleos and Perseo's navies now surrounded *The Delphis* in a wide arc, blocking its exit from the port of Talasia.

Helena rushed by, shoving Cassius aside and dashing to the front of the ship where a group of men manned the long steering oars. She stood there, leaning against the front of the ship with her eyes fixed on the battle in front of her.

"Fifteen strokes starboard!" Helena yelled, pointing to one of Perseo's ships. "We'll ram that ship first then fight our way out of here."

Of all the moves she could make, that was likely the best. Still, it wouldn't be enough. Even if *The Delphis* was the greatest ship to ever sail, it had no hope on its own. Zinnon had commissioned it to lead a navy, not to face one.

Something stirred within Cassius, and he reached out to a creature deep within the depths of the sea. In an instant, it surfaced, green tentacles bursting from the water and wrapping around the ship Helena had pointed to. The kraken dragged the vessel down with tremendous power, capsizing it before anyone could comprehend what had happened. It returned a moment later, taking the next ship in line.

"Cass?" Helena said, turning back to face him. He slunk back against the mast, falling down and curling up in a ball. The kraken continued its work, but under the weight of his failures, Cassius shut the world out. He closed his eyes, drifting off into a sleep haunted by the memory of Pollux, who he had let die by Zinnon's hand in order to regain his place with the gods.

ACT III
RISING TIDE

All is changed today
Yet tomorrow moves again
In the end, transform

Chapter Sixteen

Cassius hid himself in the hold of the ship, where he and Pollux had been imprisoned days before. *The Delphis* had escaped Ithale relatively easily once the kraken had done its work. Hidden beneath the waves, Cassius could feel it following the ship, intent on protecting it from further harm.

Even after days isolated from the outside world, Cassius still felt numb to the emptiness inside of him. Sure, Kleos' men had killed Damian, but Pollux's death was his fault. He could still see the look in Helena's eyes when he'd told her of their deaths.

The trapdoor above opened and mushroom light streamed into the cramped storage space. Daedus looked down at Cassius, a forced smile on his face. "Cassius," he said, "I don't know why I came down here. I guess I just wanted to say I'm sorry."

"No," Cassius said, "I am."

Daedus reached a hand down to Cassius. "Come to the deck. Helena is playing songs on her lyre. We're celebrating."

"How?"

"Kleos' navy finally stopped trailing us. The battle is over, Cassius. We can go home." He paused, the smile breaking on his face and moisture welling in his eyes. "Please, the crew wants to see you. We owe you our thanks."

Cassius hesitated for a moment before taking Daedus' hand and boosting himself out of the hold with magic. They climbed out of the ship's innards and onto the deck, where men and women drank wine in the light of the stars above. The crew cheered for Cassius, clapping him on the back and raising their cups in his honor. Helena sat on the floor, her back against the main mast as she plucked the strings of her lyre to play a jovial tune.

Out of instinct, Cassius looked towards the prow of the ship, where Pollux used to always stand and watch the sea. For a second, he could see Pollux there, wrapped in Zinnon's red chains. Cassius closed his eyes, blocking the image from his mind.

Helena motioned him over to sit by her. Her body leaned against his as the crew danced and sang to her song.

"It's okay, Cass," she said. "We forgive you."

"I don't."

"I know." Helena laughed under her breath. "Pollux wouldn't have either if he were in your position."

"Helena," Cassius said, wiping the sweat from his palms on his chiton, "you have to know. I could have saved him."

She shrugged, closing her eyes and breathing in the salty breeze of the seas, a tear forming in her eye. "Maybe you could have. Maybe this is all destiny. It hurts, Cass. I know it does. It hurts for me to know he's gone and that I have to lead the ship without him. I can't imagine what it's like for you to have all the power in the world, but not what you needed to save him."

"It's my fault."

"Maybe." Her song ended as the moon began to peer out from behind a group of clouds, shining silvery light on her heart shaped face. Across the deck, Daedus picked up Mya and grinned as she giggled, hugging his neck. He set her down and gestured to her in their unspoken language. Drawing magic from the Union, Cassius translated their gestures so that he could understand them.

I love you, daughter, Daedus said.

When will we be home? Mya said. *I miss my friends and my bed.*

Soon, Daedus said. He picked her back up and placed her on his shoulders. They danced into the crowd, disappearing from Cassius' view. Helena leaned her head on Cassius' shoulder, taking a break from playing songs. Her breath matched the pace of Cassius', her dark hair tumbling down his shoulder. Now that he knew that she was a descendant of Antia, the similarities were obvious. They had the same heart shaped eyes and perfect pearlescent smile.

The world froze around Cassius. Helena's breathing halted and the wind stilled. The crew became statues frozen in motion. Even *The Delphis* and the waves beneath it ceased moving. Cassius stood up, walking to the edge of the ship to see what had happened.

"Order..." Zinnon's voice said in Cassius' mind. Cassius reached out to his essence through the Union. When their souls touched, magic exploded around Cassius in waves of orange and white light. It launched him into the air, accelerating him above the clouds and into the heavens above until he was surrounded by nothing but stars and the blackness of the void.

A vague memory stirred deep within Cassius. He had been to this place before. This place deep in the heart of the universe, where magic flowed in a constant cycle, creating a current that coursed through the universe like electricity in a thunderstorm. Yes, he'd been here thousands of years ago when the gods had created Pelagios. Cassius could remember the beauty and harmony of all they had created with those flows of magic.

"Order!" Zinnon's voice thundered, erupting from the silence of space. The vision changed and Cassius saw villages burning and bands of warriors slaughtering families with streams of magic. In the wake of the destruction, a figure formed from white and orange light. The being took up one of the dead bodies lying against a wall, becoming a bald man with a curly white beard. As the figure emerged from the light, he wept at the destruction.

Cassius' vision snapped back to reality and he was back on the deck, sitting against the mast with Helena leaning against him. His palms began to sweat and his heart quickened as he tried to understand what had happened. Zinnon had sent him a vision, but why?

"Helena," Cassius said, "I saw something."

"What is it?"

"I... I don't know. I remembered things that I have forgotten." He paused, catching his breath and closing his eyes. "Helena, I think we need to go to Hestia."

"Hestia?"

He nodded. "I have to confront Zinnon. He is trying to explain himself to me, but he's wrong. We need to prove that to him."

"Why?"

"Because Pollux already proved it to me," Cassius said. "He proved to me that magic should belong to humans. As long as the gods are guarding it, mortals won't be able to."

Helena grabbed his hand. "I'll talk to the crew in the morning, but you can't go back to hiding in the hold, Cass."

"You're right," Cassius said, a shiver running down his spine.

Chapter Seventeen

A few weeks later, once Anemos, the season of gales had begun, Cassius knocked on the door to Daedus and Theora's cabin. They had been the most angry when Cassius and Helena announced that the ship would stop by Hestia before returning to Talasia. He couldn't blame them for wanting to protect their daughter and heal from the trauma that Kleos had subjected their family to, but Cassius also needed their help.

The door swung inward and Theora stood in the doorway staring at Cassius with hard eyes and messy hair. "What is it?" she said. "Come to announce another detour?"

"No." Cassius bowed his head to the woman. "I would like to bless Mya with the ability to hear. I know it's come at a far greater cost than you would have liked, but I want to help her."

Tears welled in Theora's eyes and she looked over her shoulder at Mya playing with some wooden figures that the crew had made for her. "Took you long enough," Theora said. She walked over to Mya, signing to her and grabbing her hand. Together, they joined Cassius on the main deck where Daedus already stood with Helena. Wind cut through the air, whistling over the sound of the waves as Cassius knelt down in front of Mya. Theora tapped her forward, urging her to go to Cassius. He took a deep breath and began signing to her.

Although he could understand the gestures with magic, it had taken him much longer to learn it. Daedus had spent many hours helping him practice.

Mya, Cassius said, *do you know who I am?*

You are like the god who took me, aren't you? She said, her hand movements much faster and more fluid than his.

In some ways, yes. I will not take you again though. Cassius looked up at Theora, who held a hand over her mouth. He had made it a point to hide from her that Daedus had taught him to sign. *I promise I will protect you, Mya. I will not let you be hurt by the gods again. You will be safe, happy even.*

Will I get to go home?

Soon, Cassius said, pausing for a moment. *I want to give you your hearing, Mya. I have watched you for a long time, and I have seen that you are strong. You are not burdened by your deafness. You live well even though you are not like others.*

Before replying, she looked to each of her parents, who nodded in approval. They smiled with teary eyes, joining together behind her with held hands.

Will it hurt?

No, Cassius said, *I will make it easy for you.*

Then yes, she said. *I want to hear.*

Cassius smiled and embraced her. As he held her, he drew on the Union inside of him, allowing the magic to flow into Mya gently and alter her hearing, much like he had with Antia's sight long ago. The transformation happened in seconds and ended as Mya began to tremble in fear of the new sounds. He nodded to Daedus and Theora, who knelt down to speak to her.

"Mya," Daedus said. She looked at him with wide eyes. "That is your name." He made the hand motion for it to her as he said her name over and over again.

"Mya," she said, imitating the way he said the word. It would take her time to learn the spoken language, but Cassius knew the love of her parents. They would do all that they could to help her. In many ways, the gods needed to be more like Daedus and Theora.

Cassius moved away so the parents could spend time with Mya. Helena motioned him to the front of the ship where the steering oarsmen would normally work. They'd taken a break for a few minutes to get some food. "Feeling any better?" She said as he took her side.

"No," Cassius said, reminded of the pain he held inside. "Every day is the same struggle. I wake up guilty, and I feel no more redeemed by the time I lay down to rest."

"It'll be okay, Cass. We can fix things."

"I hope so."

She pointed out to the horizon, where the darkest sliver of land had appeared. "There it is," Helena said, a hint of reverence in her voice. "Hestia, the city of gods."

"Have you ever been?" Cassius said, grabbing her hand and holding it in his.

"Only its port, but I don't count that."

"That counts. You can learn a lot about a place by its port."

She twirled around into his arms, her emerald eyes meeting his. "You have to meet people to know what a city is really like, Cass. Sure, Hestia is pretty, but what if everyone who lives there is miserable? That says a lot more about a place than its marble columns and shiny mushrooms."

"Well you've met me, and I'm technically from Hestia."

Helena laughed and pulled herself away to lean on the edge of the railing. "If all of Hestia is like you, I'll enjoy it there."

"Oh, really?"

"For sure."

In a moment of courage, Cassius touched her arm, turning her back to him. He cupped a hand on her cheek and leaned forward, kissing her as deeply as he knew how. Their lips lingered for a moment and warmth rushed through Cassius' veins. As they pulled away, Cassius found himself wondering how a human could be so beautiful.

"For a god, you're not too shabby at kissing," Helena said with a grin.

"Well," Cassius said, blood rushing to his face, "You're not too bad either. For a mortal."

A gust of wind blew by, throwing Helena's hair wildly to the side. She grimaced, untying a thin cord from her wrist to pull her hair behind her head. Anemos, the season of gales, was a sailor's dream. With unlimited wind at the sails, a ship could go almost anywhere it wanted. Of course, as the ship got closer to Hestia, the effect dampened. All of the seasons were weakened the closer they were to Hestia. The presence of the gods protected it in a way that Cassius had never fully understood.

"So what's your plan?" Cassius said to Helena.

"You'll hate it."

"Try me."

"Well, it starts with that kraken of yours. He needs a name doesn't he?"

Cassius put a hand up to his face and rubbed at his eyes. "Your entire plan is naming a kraken?"

"No!" She pretended to act offended, rolling her eyes and huffing. Eventually, she let up the act and smiled again. "But he does need one."

"Here." Cassius called to the beast with his magic. It surged from the depths, its bulbous green head poking above the waterline. Beady yellow eyes sat on the front of its face, watching Cassius and Helena carefully.

"He's beautiful." Helena reached out a hand and the kraken's tentacle emerged from the water, brushing along her fingertips. "I'll call him Kytos."

"It's a good name," Cassius said, holding her close to him by the waist. After a minute or two, Kytos descended back into the Minean Sea, bellowing a soft, melodic call to Helena. Her grin grew even wider and she closed her eyes, basking in the light of the sun as Hestia grew ever larger on the horizon.

"Now," Helena said, "do you want to hear the rest of my plan?"

Chapter Eighteen

A few hours later, when night draped its darkness around Pelagios and *The Delphis* had set down its anchors just outside of Hestia's port, Cassius blasted through the water in a current towards the port of Hestia. Both Kleos and Perseo's navies had arrived before *The Delphis*, and waved their flags high in the air for all to see. Before leaping out of the water, Cassius summoned a wave of fog from the sea. It washed in, clouding the city in a matter of minutes.

Cassius pulled himself out of the water, using magic to dry his body. Kytos stirred beneath the dock, eager for a fight. Soon enough, he would have what he wanted. Cassius wanted something different, something much more righteous. Magic for mortals.

He walked up to the gangplank of a ship, where Kleos' hoplites had brought out glowing mushrooms to try and drive away the fog. "Hey! You!" a guard yelled, grabbing Cassius from behind.

"This vessel is now under my command," Cassius said. One of Kytos' tentacles emerged from the surface of the Minean Sea, yanking the guard into the air and tossing him toward the city. The sound of his scream faded as he flew away and Cassius continued down the deck. A hoplite rushed him with a spear, but Cassius drew his xiphos and pointed at him. "I am Cassius, god of the seas, and you will obey."

"Kleos beat you already," the hoplite said.

"Tides rise and fall, my friend." Cassius lunged in, slicing the hoplite's wrist and severing an artery. The man's spear dropped to the deck of the ship and the others backed away, hands held over their mouths. Cassius floated upwards until he was at the top of the mast. He touched Kleos' red flag and it changed to a navy blue. For a moment he hovered there beside the flag, his godly eyes piercing through the fog so that he could see the marbled city of Hestia.

After a minute or two, he dropped down onto another ship. The hoplites on the ships were far more eager to fight him, but Kytos made quick work of them. All Cassius needed to do was send a message. He walked to the third ship, one of Perseo's this time. His ships were far larger and made for ramming rather than boarding.

"What are you doing?" a shadowy figure said as Cassius reached the deck of Perseo's ship. To his surprise, Phoebe had come to confront him before Perseo or Kleos. Of course, he'd seen the look in her eyes in Kleos' temple. Whatever secret Zinnon was hiding, she seemed in on it too.

"Taking back my glory as boldly as I know how." Cassius laughed. "I'm done pulling my punches. If Kleos and Perseo want war with me, they can have it."

"No, that's not it." Phoebe stepped in close, her soft scent lingering into the air next to Cassius. She paced around him, her knuckles brushing against his as she passed by. "You're angry, Cassius."

"Don't you think I deserve to be?" Cassius faced her, holding his xiphos out to the side for her to see. It wouldn't do him much good against a god, but he felt more confident having it. "I saw a vision, Phoebe. It was a memory we've lost. I think I'm starting to remember."

"Remember what?"

"The creation of Pelagios."

Phoebe's eyes narrowed and she looked around to see if anyone was listening. "Don't speak of that." The words were a hiss, biting through the cold night air.

Behind them, footsteps thumped down the dock. "Cassius!" Kleos' voice bellowed.

A thin smile stretched across Phoebe's perfect lips. "Good," she said. "I've stalled long enough." She backed away as Kleos walked up the gangplank, fully armed and ready for battle.

"Are you a fool?" Kleos said, holding his spear up to Cassius' face.

"No," Cassius said, "just foolish." He ducked beneath the spear, driving forward and shoving Kleos off the side of the ship. It happened suddenly enough that Kleos couldn't react before he tumbled over the ship's railing and into the sea below. Phoebe giggled behind Cassius and a hand grabbed him by his chiton. It pulled him backwards, lifting him up into the air.

"You!" Perseo's voice thundered. Cassius tried to wrestle his way free, but Perseo's grip was too strong for him. "How dare you attack my ships!"

"I was wondering where you were," Cassius said. He created a column of water out of the sea, blasting Perseo in the face. The god of boldness sputtered, teetering backwards and releasing his hold on Cassius. As Cassius' feet hit the deck, Kleos leapt out of the water, jabbing at Cassius with his spear.

Cassius spun to the side just as Kleos began a magical onslaught on his soul. This time, instead of caving in like he had during the attack on Talasia, Cassius pushed back. He thought of Pollux and his defiance against Zinnon. The emotions he felt for Pollux's death surged, but instead of allowing them to cripple him, they became fuel. In an instant, the magical fight between Cassius and Kleos' souls shifted and Kleos' essence crumpled against Cassius'. The god of glory fell to his knees, all color drained from his face. His mortal form seemed to flicker as if he were losing his grasp of reality.

Another essence, Zinnon, reached out to Cassius, gently beckoning him towards the center of Hestia. Zinnon sent feelings of grief and pleading, as if he were asking Cassius to come speak with him, to try and understand the lies that he had told. "No," Cassius replied through the Union, "you must see that I am done giving in."

A horn sounded in the distance and the fog began to dissipate. The crew of *The Delphis* leapt from the decks of the ship onto the backs of massive sea turtles below. The turtles carried them to the rest of Kleos and Perseo's fleets, which had already been cleared of aggressors by Kytos. They climbed the masts, taking down old flags and replacing them with Cassius' navy blue. Where the port met the city, Helena and Daedus pulled down Zinnon's banner and pulled up Cassius' seahorse banner. It was the first time in many cycles that Cassius had seen his banner without tatters.

An explosion of light shined in the sky above, turning night into day for a brief moment. A figure clad in white descended from the sky, landing on the deck of the ship where Cassius and the other three gods were fighting. "Enough!" Zinnon said. "I will have order."

"Good," Cassius said. "What are your terms of surrender?"

"My... what?"

"I beat you fair and square. If you want your dock back, you've got to give me what I want." Cassius sheathed his xiphos and folded his arms. "I need to know the secrets you've been hiding about magic all along."

Zinnon took in a deep breath, his nostrils flaring and his brow furrowed. Finally, he turned around to look into the stars glittering above. "Fine," he said. "I will show you."

Chapter Nineteen

Once again, Cassius ascended into the heavens, where the vision began again. He watched as a multitude of lights appeared from the current of magic, each of a different color and temperament. Together they created Pelagios, a floating disc of a world with a sun and moon that orbited it. The Union of their efforts and intents in the Ktisis was responsible for the beauty of all life on Pelagios. With only one of these elements it would be incomplete. Together, they made it whole. The current of magic through the universe ebbed and flowed, manifesting physically as the seasons on Pelagios. Mortals drew on that magic, using it for their own purposes.

Over time, a blackness formed on the side of Pelagios, a cancer that grew and overshadowed the land. Cassius' view focused and he saw its source. A tribe of people chanted, using magic to warp the world in unnatural ways. The gods tried to help, but from the Union there was no way to intervene. The tribe murdered people by the hundreds. Soon, it had overtaken the entirety of Pelagios, drowning it in darkness.

In an instant, Cassius' vision fuzzed and he returned to the scene of the destroyed village. Again, he saw a figure made of orange and white light appear. This time, the details were clearer. The figure drifted through the air towards the body of a man lying against a wooden shed. The barbarians who had attacked the village scalped the man and left him to die.

The orange and white being touched the corpse, traveling into it and transforming it in a burst of energy. Energy crackled as the man healed and white hair grew into a curly beard on his face. Although the skin healed on his head, it remained bald. The man gasped as life returned to his lungs. His first breaths were hasty, rushed even. He looked down at his palms, eyes wide and jaw hung.

Even though Cassius wasn't physically there, he could sense that the soul in the body was not the man who died. The figure who had appeared and inhabited it was Zinnon himself. Cassius felt Zinnon draw on the universe's magic, using it to fuel his transformation. It felt as if Zinnon were bending a reed, forcing it into the shape he wanted. If he let go of the magic, the reed would snap back into its natural shape and Zinnon would be thrust from the mortal's body.

A being of light pink light descended from the heavens, another god that had witnessed what Zinnon had done. It pulsed like a beating heart, drawing near to Zinnon. "It's okay," he said. "Find a body, take it."

The pink being found its way to a woman, who had died screaming for help. Like the body Zinnon had chosen, it transformed. This time it became the perfect, beautiful form of Phoebe. Once her transformation was completed, she found a puddle and stared at her reflection. "What have we done?" She said, turning to face Zinnon.

"We have bodies. Now, we can live among the mortals. The terror can end," Zinnon said, his voice cracking as tears formed in his eyes. "Don't you see? The only way to stop the destruction is to be the hand that tames it. We can bring order."

"We're binding up the magic," Phoebe said. "It's like… we have to maintain a constant stream of it into our bodies to keep us in this form. It's as unnatural as what the tribe is doing."

"I know." Zinnon stood up, his white chiton spotless as he stared into the horizon with golden eyes. "It's a price that needs to be paid. The tribe has used the magic for far, far too much destruction."

Phoebe nodded, trembling as she stood up and examined the remnants of violence surrounding her. Bodies littered the ground, some even draped over one another. "You're right," she said, the words soft on her lips. "This has to end. Let us call the others."

One by one, more spirits appeared, taking up bodies. The dead strewn about the town wheezed as they reawakened, becoming the vessels of gods. Cassius' vision shifted and he found himself at the edge of town. A navy blue form floated uneasily over the body of a man who had died trying to flee the village. Many would deem him a coward for leaving behind his family and friends, but for some reason, Cassius' spirit chose him.

Moisture in the air condensed into soft raindrops, washing over the corpse as Cassius invaded it. The man's hair became blonde and his body free of scars. He grew nearly a foot and a half taller. When his eyes opened, his memories began to fade. The magic could only do so much in making the gods mortal. It sacrificed his memories, protecting his physical form instead.

Zinnon emerged from a nearby street, the other gods following close behind him, rubbing their fingers along the sides of the wooden huts. "My child," he said, reaching Cassius and kneeling. Zinnon reached out a hand to help Cassius from the ground. "Let us go and take our thrones. The world awaits us."

. . .

Static electricity raised the tiny hairs on Cassius' arm as he returned to reality. Crisp air filled his lungs. A lump formed in his throat as Phoebe stared at him, tapping her foot and waiting for his response. Behind her, Helena climbed up the gangplank onto the ship, a spear in hand.

"What did you do to him?" she said, stepping between Cassius and Phoebe, holding the spear to Phoebe's chest.

The goddess raised an eyebrow and nudged the spearhead away. She laughed. "Do you think you can hurt me?"

"Maybe not," Helena said, "but I won't let you hurt him."

"Enough, Phoebe." Zinnon raised a hand. "Let Cassius think. He has seen something that only you and I remember. Allow him this time to process it."

"Cass?" Helena said, turning her head over her shoulder to glance at him. "What's wrong?"

Cassius shook his head, trying to make sense of the jumbled thoughts in his head. "Sorry, it's just..." He looked around himself. Everything he'd ever seen, ever experienced, came at the expense of the mortals. None of it would have been possible if Zinnon hadn't done what he'd done.

But he hated it.

He hated that the mortals could no longer use magic. Where would they be with its power to heal and innovate? Pollux had proven time and time again that magic could save lives. If the humans had magic, they would be able to overcome the seasons and explore new frontiers.

"You stole from them," Cassius said. He stormed over to Zinnon, yanking him away from the ship's railing. "You took magic from the humans. All so you could have a body of your own."

"It was necessary."

"It was selfish." Kytos reeled up in the water, sensing

Cassius' anger and matching it. Its massive head surfaced above the rolling sea, beady eyes locked on Zinnon. All eight of its verdant tentacles writhed in the air, grasping at the invisible breeze as it blew by. Cassius grit his teeth, releasing his hold on Zinnon's arm and balling his shaking fists at the side. It hurt to know that all this time, he'd been preventing the mortals from using magic.

"Cassius," Phoebe drawled as she drew near, her lips close to his ear. "Don't be rash. Let us help you understand."

"No." Cassius gave Kytos the mental command and it tore into the ship, yanking Zinnon into the air and slamming him back down against the water. Splinters of wood flew into the air, but time seemed to slow as Cassius spun and dove to protect Helena, propelling them to safety on another boat. "Are you okay?" He said as he set her down gently.

"Better than I would have been," she said, looking towards Cassius' banner at the entrance to the port. "I need to get into the city to help the crew. Reinforcements are coming and there's not enough of us to hold it for long."

Cassius nodded. "I'll transport you there."

"You can do that?"

"I can do almost anything." A pit formed in his stomach as he realized that for each miracle he performed, a father like Daedus lost his chance to heal his daughter. The gods took that freedom from him. Everything bad that had happened to Daedus wouldn't have occurred if it weren't for Zinnon's choice to bind the magic.

At that moment, Cassius realized the magnitude of what it would take to restore the state of magic to what it once was. All of the gods, including him, would have to give up their bodies. They'd lose their ability to experience the world and interact with humans. Cassius would lose Helena and the crew of *The Delphis*, who he had come to love so much.

Zinnon exploded from the water, shooting into the air

and blasting a beam of white energy into Kytos' face. The beast bellowed, diving beneath the water, but Zinnon chased him.

Cassius only smiled. If Zinnon wanted a fight, he'd have to choose somewhere else. The seas were Cassius' to rule.

Chapter Twenty

A current rushed around Cassius as he darted through the water. Forests of kelp grew from the sandy seafloor, illuminated by Zinnon's aura as he hunted Kytos. Cassius would not let him harm the kraken. Fury pulsed in his veins as he whipped around a coral, splitting a school of fish and finally laying eyes on Zinnon as he ducked under the hull of a ship. Luckily, Kytos was escaping to deeper waters, where it would have more space to get away.

Cassius clenched his fist, increasing the water pressure around Zinnon. The seas caved in on him and he sputtered, grabbing the sides of his head and crumpling into a ball. Cassius accelerated, releasing the pressure and slamming into Zinnon just as the pressure released. The god went flying out of the water, and Cassius followed him into the sky, snatching him out of the air.

Only this time, Zinnon reacted, touching Cassius' soul and putting up a barrier to the Union. Magic disappeared from Cassius and he transformed into his mortal form while Zinnon flew away. For a second, he hung in the air, still as can be. Then his body lurched and his limbs flailed as he plummeted towards the sea.

In the instant before his body hit the water's surface, his perspective warped and he found himself standing in front of Zinnon's temple inside of the city. A second later, Zinnon

appeared beside him. "I had hope in you, Cassius. Why can't you just do what's right?"

"Right?" Cassius said. "You stole from the mortals."

"I'm protecting them."

Cassius scoffed, shaking his head and chuckling. "Then answer one last question. If you're stopping me from using magic, then how do I still have a body? What binds my essence to this form?"

"Why does it matter?"

"Because that would mean there's a way," Cassius said. "A way for us to have bodies without using magic."

"No." Zinnon closed his eyes and began walking into the temple. "It doesn't work like that. I only block your physical form from using magic, not your essence."

Cassius rushed after him, panting and trying everything he could to think of a solution. As much as he wanted the mortals to have access to magic, he didn't want to give up his body. He wanted to live among them.

Inside the temple's atrium, the other gods formed an arc around a brazier of technicolor mushrooms. Cassius began to wonder how he'd convince them all of what he'd seen. They'd never help Cassius if they didn't understand.

"Back to a mortal?" Kleos said, chuckling under his breath. "Now we'll see who wins a fight."

Over and over again, Cassius cycled Zinnon's words through his mind, trying to make sense of them and find a way to use them to show the gods the vision he'd seen. Without his magic, he was nothing compared to their power. Cassius' essence could use magic, but his body couldn't.

He had to give up his body. It was the only way Cassius knew of. In his pure form, he could access the Union and show them the vision Zinnon had given them. Then, they'd understand why they needed to give up their power and join him. It would hurt, but it was the only way.

Cassius closed his eyes, taking in his last breath of air before he mentally severed the attachment his soul had to his body.

He watched as his body fell lifeless to the ground, losing its color and disintegrating into dust.

Power surged and Cassius felt himself become one with the universe. He felt every shift in the ocean's current and became every seagull flying along the seashore. Unlimited power rested in him as his essence returned to that place of stars that he'd seen in the vision.

In this place, the Union felt more than a part of Cassius. He was a part of it, just as it was a part of him. The other gods felt so distant, though the familiarity of their presence lingered. "My siblings," Cassius said, his voice more a command of his power than words, "see what I have seen."

At once, he showed all of the gods the vision that he had seen. Zinnon struggled against it, but in his mortal form he could not overpower Cassius' will. They all watched as Zinnon took up a human body. Cassius shared what he had learned about the magic, and his experience on *The Delphis*. As best as he could, he showed them Daedus and Theora's love for Mya, using it to prove to them that humanity needed magic. They deserved the choice to use it as they wished.

Another god returned to the Union, pleading alongside Cassius for the others to join them. Eventually, light appeared all around as the gods began to give up their mortal forms. For a moment, Kleos hesitated, still angry with Cassius for all he'd done. Cassius extended his essence, showing Kleos the glory that mortals could have through their independence. Kleos joined, leaving only Phoebe and Zinnon physically present on Pelagios.

"They can't be trusted to use magic," Zinnon said. He and Phoebe still stood in the temple, alone but for the luminescent mushrooms.

"Neither can we. Where there is power, it can be corrupted." Cassius' intent became one with the rest of the gods.

"There is a way," Zinnon said, joining hands with Phoebe. "We can make a governing system. A way that some humans can use magic, but others can't."

"They must all have the opportunity," Cassius and the others said. "But we can change the way they access it."

"How?"

The other gods turned their will to Cassius, and he showed Zinnon a vision of Mya using hand gestures to speak to her parents and friends. It shifted, and Cassius portrayed an image of a man using hand signs to shape and direct the flows of magic, accessing the universe's magic to protect a group of people from the sun's rays during Kalokeri.

Phoebe's essence returned to the Union, her perfected body disappearing from the temple. After a moment of hesitancy, Zinnon followed, agreeing to Cassius' terms.

Together, the gods set to work, changing the very fabric of reality so that the mortals could access the magic, but only under the right conditions. Cassius defined hand signs that would purify water for drinking or call great beasts like Kytos from the sea. Phoebe's essence created spells of emotion, and the deities of seasons made ways for the mortals to take control of the seasons.

When the work was finished, Cassius found himself watching Helena return to the crew of *The Delphis* in Hestia. She led them back to the ship and took charge. Before the remnants of Kleos' army could reach them, *The Delphis* had made it out of the port. In only a week, they arrived home in Talasia.

Several days later, Helena sat on the beach, watching the sun as it set on the horizon. Nearby, Daedus and Theora taught Mya to write by etching their fingers in the sand. Several times that day, Helena had gone to Cassius' hut to look for him. He wanted so bad to return to her, to tell her why the gods had vanished. Even if it were just for a few minutes, Cassius wanted to hold her in his arms again.

But he couldn't. The gods had made a choice, and it was only right that they uphold it. He drifted away, his attention returning to the Union. Although Cassius no longer had the physical ability to smile, he remembered the feelings of happiness he'd felt training with Damian and speaking with Pollux. His experiences with a body became a treasured part of his essence as Cassius, god of the seas, extended into the eternities, keeping a watchful eye on Pelagios as waves churned and tides rose.

Epilogue

Mya, oracle of the gods, was reminded of a sickening fact as she stood in front of Emperor Isyphus, ruler of the Hestian Empire. People did not like what she had to say. Unfortunately, she had to say it anyway. Even now as she stood among white robed advisors in one of the imperial palace's marble hearing chambers, Mya could hear the whispers at the edge of her mind begging to be set free.

Fifty-four cycles ago when Cassius gave Mya the ability to hear, he bestowed upon her something else as well. Her mind bore the weight of prophecies—tellings of the future that coalesced in her own consciousness and compelled her to set them free. She questioned every day whether Cassius' act had been one of graciousness or cruelty.

"Word of your talent has come to me from the far and wide places of Pelagios, oracle," Emperor Isyphus said, his dark hair adorned with a golden laurel. He was young, perhaps still a teenager. Isyphus had taken the throne after the death of his father only two seasons ago. "They say that you have saved lives and foretold the deaths of others. Tell me, do they speak the truth?"

Mya pursed her lips in thought before giving her reply. When she did speak, she spoke not with pride but trepidation. "If the tales are as remarkable as you suggest, emperor, then yes, I imagine there is no fault in what you have been told."

Isyphus grinned. Murmurs passed through the politicians and nobility sitting in the elevated levels of seating that surrounded the chamber. A knot formed in Mya's stomach. She had observed the same reactions in countless audiences before. With every rumor and story that passed of her ability, it escaped her grasp even further. People did not understand what she could do, and people blamed her for it foolish though that was.

Emperor Isyphus stood, his toga draping to the floor. A violet sash emblazoned with a golden seahorse wrapped across his body. He glanced at one of the advisors standing nearby writing the conversation on a scroll. Once the advisor finished writing with a nod, the emperor's cunning eyes settled on Mya standing in the center of the court. "Would you prophesy to us today?"

Dread settled over Mya, pressing down upon her shoulders. She cast her gaze to the floor where her face reflected in the polish. Upon looking at herself, Mya couldn't help but see what hid within. She allowed the whispers to come to the forefront of her mind. Her eyes began to glow a vibrant yellow.

Survivor...

Champion...

Titan...

Creases formed in her forehead as Mya concentrated on discerning the voices. They rasped, giving way before her will until only one remained. Sweat formed at Mya's temple as she opened her mouth and set the voice free. It rushed forth, gone as quickly as Mya spoke it. Once finished, she slumped, her body weary and eyelids drooping.

Above, the emperor squinted at Mya. Beside him the scribe finished writing her words and handed Emperor

Isyphus a scroll. He read the prophecy once more then descended to the ground level where Mya stood. "What is the meaning of this?"

So the emperor wasn't different from anyone else that Mya had prophesied for. "I can only interpret as you can."

"These are your words," the emperor said. His face lost any pretense of kindness.

Mya forced herself to stand taller. "I speak only what I hear. I do not choose."

The advisors whispered. The prophecy itself didn't matter to Mya now. She was never in so much danger as in the moments after a delivery. What people did not understand, they feared, and when it came to matters of the future, Mya carried the blame.

"How is this done?" Emperor Isyphus stared at Mya with cold eyes.

Mya knew then that she needed to escape. Isyphus did not like what she said, and if she could not explain it, then he would find a way to punish her. Mya's fingers twitched, preparing to Sign. "When I was a child, the gods bestowed upon me this gift. It is not something others can replicate."

"You would keep your ability a secret?"

Fire coursed through Mya's veins. Others had attacked her before, but none so powerful as the emperor. He was a talented magos, and by his command Mya could be cast into prison or executed without a second thought.

"I wish it were simpler," Mya said, loud enough that the entire room would hear. "Let us make peace, and I will leave."

Isyphus scowled and turned around. He waved to the advisors then pointed to the middle of the room. "Come. Leave your parchment."

They did as he said, gathering in the middle of the chamber in front of the emperor. Dread seeped into Mya's very bones. Even the voices quieted before the looming darkness of the emperor. He raised his hands, and twisted his fingers in a single violent Sign. A crack formed in the ceiling, sending an echo through the room.

Mya's heart twisted. "No!" She started to Sign, but there was nothing to be done.

The ceiling capsized, raining down chunks of stone. The emperor turned and tackled Mya, using magic to propel them away from the falling debris. Screams echoed through the chamber until the crash snuffed them out. A cloud of dust billowed, burning at Mya's throat and eyes. She threw the emperor off of her and rushed over to the rubble. A quick Sign tossed away a boulder. Beneath lay a pile of mangled bodies.

Of all who had witnessed the prophecy, only Mya and the emperor survived. Her pulse thundered, and Mya felt as though electricity were arcing through her body. She looked over her shoulder as the doors to the chamber opened and a pair of legionarii entered. "Emperor! Are you safe?"

The emperor crawled toward his guards. "She killed them," he said. "Arrest her!"

The legionarii strode past the fallen emperor and drew their gladii, straight edged blades gleaming against the glow of mushrooms. "Let us see your hands," one said.

Trembling, Mya raised her hands. She was being framed. The emperor wanted to cover up the prophecy because of whatever he had interpreted from it. Mya couldn't help but feel that she'd known this was coming.

As the guards stepped close, she made a quick Sign, drawing magic from her surroundings to create a gust of wind that pushed the guards over. She ran past the emperor and into the palace's grand hallway. A cacophony of shouts and clamoring sounded behind her, but Mya blurred past torches attached to the walls.

Outside, Mya ducked into an alleyway to catch her breath.

She wove her way through the city toward the port where navy banners hung. A horn bellowed from the direction of the palace. Isyphus was calling the city legion to arms. Mya didn't doubt that he could have stopped her in the palace, but he hadn't. She knew the emperor to be a cunning man. Even her escape would serve a purpose.

A seagull cawed, floating down from the sky and landing on a post ahead. It stared at Mya with beady eyes. Mya ignored it as she walked past, but the bird flew to the end of the alleyway where it rejoined the main street. "Away with you." She ducked her head and turned down the street where a crowd rushed to and fro.

Pain shot up her leg, and Mya looked down at the seagull hitting her sandaled heel with its beak. It turned the other way and hopped a few steps before looking over its wing to Mya.

She scrunched her eyebrows. Was the bird trying to lead her? The season was not Teras, so it would be near impossible for any magos to control it by magical means. Even Mya, in her decades of experience, struggled with off season magic. She ignored the bird and continued on the path to the port when it pecked at her foot another time. Mya kicked at it. The bird sidehopped then tilted its head at her. It squawked and shuffled off in the other direction.

Mya huffed. As she was about to begin walking again, she saw a legionarii century marching in her direction, ordering citizens off the thoroughfare. She swore beneath her breath then spun back toward the seagull. "Fine," she said beneath her breath. If the bird wanted her dead, it wouldn't have tried to lead her away.

Trusting the seagull with her very life, Mya navigated Hestia. With each minute that passed, people returned to their homes and the streets became more empty. The seagull led her parallel to the coast but away from the port where her ship lay. Were the sailors safe or had the emperor ordered for their arrest too? Mya considered returning, but no magic could stop an entire legion. If she turned herself in, it would save the lives of her sailors. Why should Mya escape when they didn't?

Mya's path opened up to a silent beach at the end of the port where waves rolled in and cast foam over the sand. The seagull landed and sat, staring at Mya once more but offering no further direction. She collapsed to her knees, legs weak from so long fleeing. "Why here?" She looked at the navy banners hanging over the port. "I should be there. If not to stop them from hurting others, then to make a hopeless stand."

But instead she'd followed a bird.

The whispers at the edge of Mya's mind closed in, speaking of destinies and fates that belonged to everyone but herself. They were a relentless clamor of every dream and nightmare that would ever come to pass. It was Mya's curse, forced upon her at the whim of a god desperate to prove he was anything but a coward.

"Mya!" Came a voice born not of her foresight. A voice she had heard before but did not remember. It spoke with clarity and power like the rushing of a riptide. Mya cast her eyes upward but found no source to the words. Even the seagull had left her alone. "Mya! *Be not afraid.*"

On the horizon, a trireme appeared from behind a peninsula. A polished bronze ram jutted out from its hull, gleaming against the rays of the sun. A hundred oars grasped at the waves of the Minean Sea and propelled the ship forward. Above its masts, a flock of seagulls flew in a cloud of magic that shimmered and warped the air.

Mya knew it to be the *Delphis*, the legendary trireme of Cassius, god of the seas and magic. Its first voyage had been to rescue her from the god Kleos when she had been kidnapped and held ransom as a girl. The ship disappeared many cycles ago when she was still young, but now it moved toward her at unparalleled speed. Mya's heart thundered as she ran into the surf. When the ship neared, she made a quick Sign to summon an updraft that propelled her up and onto the deck where a crew awaited her.

"Oracle!" Someone said, coming to her side and grabbing her. "How did you survive?"

Mya looked up. The man was Tiphys, trierarch of the ship Mya had used to come to Hestia. Surrounding her were hundreds of men and women in loose fitting sailors garb. There were far more people than should be on the top deck if the trireme was moving. Who was manning the oars? The whole ship felt as though it were surrounded by a mist of energy. The magic here was tangible, and Mya reached out a hand, certain she could touch it without even a Sign.

"Mya?" Tiphys said.

"It sails itself, doesn't it?" she said. The *Delphis* turned away from the city of Hestia.

Tiphys nodded. "There's a magos commanding it." He pointed to the prow of the ship where an unfamiliar woman stood, dark hair streaming behind her head. "She won't speak to us."

Mya nodded and then crossed the deck to the woman. "Did you save us?"

The woman looked to Mya then pointed to her ear. She raised her hands and signed to communicate, something Mya hadn't done in many cycles now. Snake tattoos spiraled around her forearms. *Oracle*, the woman said, *I am Erinye, servant of the gods. You are blessed to have escaped the emperor's wrath.*

Mya signed her reply. *Thanks to you.*

Thanks to him. Erinye pointed behind Mya to where the seagull from earlier rested on the railing.

The whispered prophecies in Mya's mind seemed to calm with understanding. *Cassius*, she signed.

You inspired him.

Mya held back a snide comment. The gods kidnapped her, and then bestowed upon her the curse of foresight. They abandoned Pelagios, leaving behind Mya's own sign language as the means of access to their magic. Every time they tried to help, Mya's life only became worse.

Erinye leaned over the railing. *You are upset. Understand that the gods made their choices for our good.*

Their intentions may have been good, but they have still done harm.

Erinye's face remained expressionless. *You know better than most the burden of power.*

She was right. Mya lived every day under the weight of her gift. What must it be to have power that extends into eternity? In times before, she had wished that the gods were still present to lead them. Without them, the people of Pelagios were lost.

The gods made mistakes, Erinye said. *Just as you and I have. Now they have made a choice that is right for humankind. That does not make it easy, but you can be a light. You can guide us.*

Sweat formed on Mya's nape. *How?*

Trust your gifts. Trust Cassius. He will show the way.

Mya looked out into the horizon, and the seagull flitted over onto her shoulder. Even though in the moment all was lost, a sense of peace overcame Mya. It was a feeling that she remembered before from when Cassius granted her hearing.

A voice emerged from the back of her mind, and Mya began to speak words of hope. She prophesied a future filled with light, one blessed by the choices of god and man alike. When she finished, the seagull hopped down. The depth of lightness in its eyes faded away, and it flew off to rejoin its flock.

GLOSSARY OF PELAGIOS

–GODS–

DEITIES OF EXPERIENCE

Zinnon - Enlightenment
Phoebe - Passion
Kleos - Glory
Perseo - Boldness
Libertas - Freedom
Empisto - Trust

DEITIES OF SEASONS

Thriamvos
Kalokeri
Anemos
Teras
Kheima
Sapila

DEITIES OF NATURE

Cassius - Seas
Oura - Skies
Gios - Earth
Ampelos - Flora
Psari - Fauna
Ilios - Light

–Seasons–

The seasons of Pelagios are a manifestation of the current of magic that flows through the universe. Each season is six weeks long, and a cycle represents the completion of all six seasons.

Thriamvos (The Season of Triumph)
The most peaceful season. Typically, this is when crops such as grain and olives are harvested. Magic is at its most powerful during this season

Kalokeri (The Season of Sun)
The hottest season. Exposure to the sun causes burns that do not fade in intensity without magical healing. Also, powerful heat waves occur at random intervals.

Anemos (The Season of Gales)
A season characterized by extreme winds and storms. Cyclones and hurricanes are especially common during this season.

Teras (The Season of Beasts)
During this season, creatures of all kinds are born. Most notable are monsters such as the hydra and the cyclops.

Kheima (The Season of Ice)
The coldest season. Temperatures across Pelagios plummet and icebergs form in the Minean Sea.

Sapila (The Season of Rot)
Magic is the least abundant during this season. Without its touch, diseases spread and crops wither. This is the deadliest of all seasons.

–Xiphos Forms–

Stasi (Stance Form)
A defensive form. Based on taking a stance and reacting to the moves of your
  opponent.

Coros (Dance Form)
An offensive form. The user constantly maneuvers and changes positions,
  fighting at their own tempo.

About the Author

Jaxon Charlton grew up in a family of educators who instilled in him a love for reading. He began writing in the third grade and has accumulated dozens of stories and worlds since then. When Jaxon is not reading or writing, he enjoys playing basketball, learning about animals, and traveling. He is also burdened with the care of a mischievous cat, who loves to tear up furniture and steal his food.

instagram.com/authorjaxoncharlton

Christian Ladd Hall Scholarship for Mental Health Advocacy

Christian Hall was a close friend to me and my family and a beta reader for an older project of mine. Christian struggled throughout his life with mental illness. Christian passed in July 2022. In his honor, Psi Chi, the international honor society in psychology, founded the Christian Ladd Hall Scholarship for Mental Health Advocacy.

A portion of all proceeds from *Cassius, God of the Seas* will be donated to the scholarship in Christian's memory.